Merrily We Dance and Sing

(Or "The Naughty Boy")

Book & Lyrics
Billy Van Zandt & Jane Milmore

Music
Billy Van Zandt, Jane Milmore,
& Ed Alton

A SAMUEL FRENCH ACTING EDITION

SAMUEL
FRENCH

FOUNDED 1830

SAMUELFRENCH.COM
SAMUELFRENCH-LONDON.CO.UK

ISBN 978-0-573-70429-1
www.SamuelFrench.com
www.SamuelFrench-London.co.uk

FOR PRODUCTION ENQUIRIES

UNITED STATES AND CANADA
Info@SamuelFrench.com
1-866-598-8449

UNITED KINGDOM AND EUROPE
Plays@SamuelFrench-London.co.uk
020-7255-4302

Each title is subject to availability from Samuel French, depending upon
country of performance. Please be aware that *MERRILY WE DANCE
AND SING (OR "THE NAUGHTY BOY")* may not be licensed by Samuel
French in your territory. Professional and amateur producers should
contact the nearest Samuel French office or licensing partner to verify
availability.

No one shall make any changes in this title(s) for the purpose of production. No part of this book may be reproduced, stored in a retrieval system, or transmitted in any form, by any means, now known or yet to be invented, including mechanical, electronic, photocopying, recording, videotaping, or otherwise, without the prior written permission of the publisher. No one shall upload this title(s), or part of this title(s), to any social media websites.

For all enquiries regarding motion picture, television, and other media rights, please contact Samuel French.

MUSIC USE NOTE

Licensees are solely responsible for obtaining formal written permission from copyright owners to use copyrighted music in the performance of this play and are strongly cautioned to do so. If no such permission is obtained by the licensee, then the licensee must use only original music that the licensee owns and controls. Licensees are solely responsible and liable for all music clearances and shall indemnify the copyright owners of the play(s) and their licensing agent, Samuel French, against any costs, expenses, losses and liabilities arising from the use of music by licensees. Please contact the appropriate music licensing Billy Van Zandt, Jane Millmore & Ed Altonity in your territory for the rights to any incidental music.

RENTAL MATERIALS

An orchestration consisting of **Piano Vocal Score**, **Vocal Chorus Books**, and **Performance Tracks** will be loaned two months prior to the production ONLY on the receipt of the Licensing Fee quoted for all performances, the rental fee and a refundable deposit. Please contact Samuel French for perusal of the music materials as well as a performance license application.

IMPORTANT BILLING AND CREDIT REQUIREMENTS

If you have obtained performance rights to this title, please refer to your licensing agreement for important billing and credit requirements.

MERRILY WE DANCE AND SING (OR THE NAUGHTY BOY) was first produced by Mark Fleming and presented at the Henderson Theatre in Lincroft, New Jersey on May 20, 1994. The performance was directed by Billy Van Zandt and Art Neill, with sets and lights by Mark Fleming, costumes by Kitty Cleary, sound by BJ Smith, music arrangements and orchestrations by Ed Alton, musical direction by Michael Kroll, chroeography by Art and Jackie Neill, scenic art by Amy Bingler and photography by Danny Sanchez. The Production Stage Manager was Sue Kulinyi, the Stage Manager was Neil Murphy, and the Technical Director was Tom Levier. The cast was as follows:

LORETTA PEAMAN/SWEET CARNATION'S NAN . . . . Sherle Tallent

CHUCK PEAMAN/MAYOR . . . . Tom Frascatore

SERGEANT TAGGERT . . . . Michael Kroll

POLICEMAN #1 . . . . Greg Schweers

POLICEMAN #2 . . . . Bob Thompson

BERNIE LUDLOE . . . . Mark Fleming

PETEY/THE FOOL . . . . Glenn Jones

MICKEY/THE NAUGHTY BOY . . . . Billy Van Zandt

COREY/SWEET CARNATION . . . . Jane Milmore

BROCK/THE MAJOR-GENERAL . . . . .Art Neill

JACK "JACKIE" BALDO . . . . .Jack Ryan

With:

Frank Andrews

Sharon Coyle

Ian Gonzalez

Maureen Milmore

Jackie Neill

Doris Villars

Sally Winters

CHARACTERS

CHUCK PEAMAN, playing the role of the Mayor of Himm

LORETTA PEAMAN, playing the role of Sweet Carnation's Nan

MICKEY, playing the role of the Naughty Boy

COREY, playing the role of Sweet Carnation

BROCK, playing the role of the Major-General

PETEY, playing the role of the Fool

JACK "JACKIE" BALDO, Escaped Mental Patient

SERGEANT TAGGERT, the real thing

TWO POLICEMEN, also real

BERNIE LUDLOE, the show's composer and conductor

CHORUS BOYS AND GIRLS (at least four)

MUSICAL NUMBERS

ACT ONE

"Overture/Happy Hamlett of Himm" . . . . . **MAYOR, THE FOOL, SWEET CARNATION'S NAN, CHORUS**

"A Naughty Boy Am I" . . . . **NAUGHTY BOY** and **CHORUS GIRLS**

"They Call Me Sweet Carnation" . . . . **SWEET CARNATION**

"Once Upon a Time" . . . . **SWEET CARNATION** and **NAUGHTY BOY**

"I'm Sweet Carnation's Nan" . . . **SWEET CARNATION'S NAN, CHORUS GIRLS**

"I Am First an Englishman" . . . . **NAUGHTY BOY** and **TOWNSFOLK**

"I Am a Soldier" . . . . **THE MAJOR-GENERAL**

"A Plan, a Scheme" . . . . **MAYOR, THE FOOL,** and **TOWNSFOLK**

"Once Upon a Time (Reprise)" . . . . . **MAJOR GENERAL** and **THE FOOL**

"There's Going to Be a Wedding" . . . . **CHORUS**

"There's Going to Be Two Weddings" . . . . **CHORUS**

"Always See It Through" . . . . **FULL COMPANY**

ACT TWO

Act Two Entr'acte

"There's Going to Be Two Weddings" . . . . . **SWEET CARNATION'S NAN, MAYOR, CHORUS**

"The Lord of the Hamlet" . . . . **COMPANY**

"The Calling of Love" . . . . **NAUGHTY BOY**

"It's All in the Chase" . . . . **MAJOR GENERAL, NAUGHT BOY, MAYOR, THE FOOL**

"On the Run or On the Lam" . . . . . **SERGEANT, PATROLMEN, CHORUS**

"Finale (Medley)" . . . . **COMPANY**

ACT ONE

(Pre-show, in theater lobby: local policemen wander through the lobby with xerox photos of a deranged-looking bearded man [JACK aka JACKIE BALDO], an escapee from the nearest state mental institute. The policemen ask theater-goers if they have seen the man in question, hand out the photo/flyers, and/ or ask them to call if they see anything suspicious.)

(Lights: houselights down)

(A spotlight hits LORETTA Peaman, a matron of the arts and President of the Monmouth County Drama League. She is dressed in a nanny's costume, like something out of Pirates of Penzance.*)*

LORETTA. Good evening. I am Loretta Peaman, President of the Monmouth County Drama League.

(She bows appropriately for a small spattering of applause.)

I bet you didn't recognize me dressed like this because I'm in my costume. Welcome to our annual production. Tonight we are pleased to present an original operetta titled "The Naughty Boy" or "If I Had It to Do All Over Again, I'd Do It All Over You." Tonight's show is written by our own Bernie Ludloe! Let's hear it for Bernie. Whoop. Whoop. Whoop. Sorry, girls. He's taken. Be still my beating heart.

(voice from backstage)

CHUCK. Get off the stage, Loretta!

LORETTA. Before we begin we'd like to thank two people – without whom this production would not be possible.

7

Of course, I'm talking about Tom & Amy Bingler. Where are they? Stand up. Tom, where are you two?

(Spotlight hits two unsuspecting people in the audience.)

Tom & Amy painted our lovely scenery. Nice dress, Amy. Macy's having another sale?

(voice from backstage)

CHUCK. Psst. Move it, Loretta. Let's go.

LORETTA. And of course you all know my husband Chuck. You may not recognize him in the show tonight – because he has hair! The first time I saw him in his costume I said "Who the hell is that?" Oh, the laughs we've had on him. And now, without further ado...

(A policeman [SERGEANT TAGGERT] steps out onto the stage. LORETTA is surprised. Two PATROLMEN block the exits.)

Oh!

SERGEANT. Excuse me, Ma'am. Ladies and gentleman, Bob Taggert, Middletown Police. We don't want to alarm anyone, but...

(handing LORETTA a flyer)

...there seems to be an escaped patient from the New Jersey Home for the Criminally Insane loose in the area. Jack "aka Jackie" Baldo.

If you spot him, please remain seated, remain calm and let a trained professional handle the situation. Just hope to God he doesn't crack your neck like a dried twig – like he did to that poor... Uh. Never mind. I repeat. Stay calm. And if you need us, my men and I will be in the lobby armed with guns. Enjoy the show.

(They exit down the aisles into the lobby. LORETTA continues.)

LORETTA. Uh... Well, you heard the Officer. Sit back. And relax. And remember...we have a strict no refund policy. My mother at the box office will back me up on that.

CHUCK. *(off)* Jesus, Mary and Joseph, will you get off the freaking stage!

LORETTA. And as I said to my husband Chuck before we drove over here tonight...

> *(From underneath the stage curtain, LORETTA is yanked by her feet. She falls on her face and is dragged backstage, arms outstretched. After a beat, she reappears through the curtain adjusting herself, trying to pretend nothing happened.)*

And now... "The Naughty Boy" by Bernie Ludloe.

> *(She exits through the curtain. A spotlight hits far stage left and BERNIE LUDLOE, local musical genius, appears. He bows to the audience then crosses to the steps leading down to the pit. The spotlight follows him, but stops at the top of the stairs. BERNIE falls down the staircase in the dark, in a painful crashing thud. After a beat, the spotlight picks him up on the floor. He rises, tries to save his dignity and crosses to his music stand. He places the score on the stand, then unveils an iPhone player with speakers.)*

> *(He presses "play" and the overture begins. He conducts it dramatically.)*

MUSIC CUE #1: "OVERTURE/HAPPY HAMLET OF HIMM"

> *(The curtain opens to reveal a typical Gilbert & Sullivan-like town square. Stage right is a tall house with a second story window. Up stage center is a backdrop of snow covered alps. Stage left, there is another house. All the painting is cartoony and amateurish. The town square is filled with townspeople – "the CHORUS" along with the MAYOR – a jovial soul [LORETTA's husband CHUCK] who speaks in a happy weinerschnitzel*

> *man accent,* **SWEET CARNATION'S NAN** — *an old crone* (**LORETTA**) *who speaks in a thick cockney accent. All other cast members speak without accents. As the curtain opens, it catches on the skirt of a* **CHORUS GIRL**. *She squeals and runs offstage in her corset and stockings to retrieve her skirt, put it back on, and get back into place as the intro is played.*)

ALL. *(bright and gay)*

WE'RE THE HAPPY HAMLET OF HIMM!

MAYOR.

I'M THE HAPPY MAYOR!

TOWNSFOLK.

THAT'S HIM!

ALL.

LIFE IS SWEET AND OH SO JOYOUS,
NOTHING HERE WILL E'ER ANNOY US.
WE'RE THE HAPPY HAMLET OF HIMM!
WE'RE THE HAPPY HAMLET OF HIMM,

CHORUS BOY #1.

I AM JIMMY.

MAYOR.

HIYA, JIM.

CHORUS BOY #1. Bon Jour!

ALL.

WE'RE CONTENT WITH BREAD THAT'S BROWN,
WE DRINK ALE AND MARCH AROUND.
WE'RE THE HAPPY HAM-LE-ET...
OF HIMM...!

MAYOR.

NOT "HAM."

THE FOOL.

NOT "HEM."

SWEET CARNATION'S NAN.

NOT "HUM."

ALL.

BUT "HIMM...!"

> *(At conclusion of this and every other number, the actors take small quick vaudeville-type bows, then pose back into character.)*

MAYOR. Ya ya. I'm the happy Mayor of Himm. The happiest hamlet in all the land. My duty is to serve the people. And serve them I do. With a civil tongue, too. After all, I am a civil servant, you know. Oh how I want everyone in my village to be happy and gay like I am.

> *(A **CHORUS BOY** laughs at him.)*

Shut up.

> *(continuing on)*

I shall never rest so long as there's even but one poor soul who remains unfulfilled in my hamlet.

SWEET CARNATION'S NAN. I'm unfulfilled.

MAYOR. Get away from me, you old goat.

> *(aside)*

Sweet Carnation's toothless old Nan. An elderly servant of Sweet Carnation's late parents who took Carnation in as her own after her parents were washed overboard in a tragic boating mishap. Gives the phrase "Wave goodbye" a whole new meaning around here. Anyway, Nan has but two goals in life. To provide Sweet Carnation with a life of eternal bliss and to become the wife of the mayor – the mayor being yours truly. The former is a selfless act of love and devotion. The latter, a fate I wouldn't wish on a dog.

THE FOOL. *(posing with his leg up)* I'm a dog.

MAYOR. "Twiddles" – the town fool. What are you doing fool?

THE FOOL. Questions. Always questions. To be or not to be...

MAYOR. Hey. We'll have none of that in this Hamlet. Anyway, off with you. And now I must go cut a ribbon and drink a lot of ale.

MUSIC CUE #2: "PLAYOFF MUSIC"

(As the **MAYOR** *and* **THE FOOL** *exit stage right. The* **CHORUS GIRLS** *squeal with delight as they look off left, pointing.)*

CHORUS GIRL #1. Look! It's the Naughty Boy from the country next door!

(The **GIRLS** *squeal with delight.)*

CHORUS GIRL #1. And he's coming this way!

MUSIC CUE #3: "A NAUGHTY BOY AM I – THE VAMP STARTS"

(The **GIRLS** *squeal again, as the* **NAUGHTY BOY** *enters, clog-dancing, in all his alpine splendor, from stage right. The* **GIRLS** *adjust their looks. the* **NAUGHTY BOY** *wears liederhausen and knee socks, an alpine hat with a tall feather, and has blonde hair – much like a Carol Channing wig. The actor also wears his horn-rimmed glasses.)*

NAUGHTY BOY.

A NAUGHTY BOY AM I,
WITH RAPTURE OVERFLOWING.
I KISS THE GIRLS,
THEIR CURLS ARE PEARLS,
AND THEN I MUST BE GOING.

(The **NAUGHTY BOY** *kisses the* **GIRLS** *one by one as the* **CHORUS** *sings – except when he comes to the older lady* **CHORUS GIRL**, *he merely shakes her hand.)*

GIRLS.

WITH RAPTURE OVERFLOWING.
ONE KISS AND HE'LL BE GOING.
ONE KISS AND GONE,
HE'S ON SOME BLONDE,

AND YES HE MUST BE GOING.

> (*The* **NAUGHTY BOY** *dances behind them, goosing all. The last one he gooses is the older lady, after which he looks down at his wrist.*)

NAUGHTY BOY. Hey, my watch!
A NAUGHTY BOY AM I,
ENCHANTED BY THE PRETTIES.
I KISS THEIR LIPS.
THEIR HIPS ARE PIPS.
I EVEN LOVE THEIR SMI-ILES.

GIRLS.
ENCHANTED BY US PRETTIES.
HE EVEN LOVES OUR SMI-ILES.
HE'LL KISS OUR LIPS.
OUR HIPS ARE PIPS.
HE NEVER WANTS TO QUITTIES!

NAUGHTY BOY. Quick, girls. To the garden! You know how I love to go down to the flower bed and look up your bloomers.

> (*The* **GIRLS** *all cheer. The* **NAUGHTY BOY** *exits stage right with all the* **GIRLS** *kissing him, clog-dancing. After a beat, the older lady* **CHORUS GIRL** *is shoved back onstage and exits upstage left dejected, turning back to give him an italian salute as she exits.*)

> (**SWEET CARNATION'S NAN** *enters from the house stage right.*)

SWEET CARNATION'S NAN. Ow, me bleedin' 'ands from me bloomin' chores. Ow, life in this bleedin' Bavarian 'amlet is rough on an old sod like me, it is.

CHORUS GIRL #1. (*Off – on mike*) There goes Loretta with that stupid cockney accent, again.

CHORUS GIRL #2. (*Off – on mike*) Somebody want to tell her the show takes place in the Bavarian alps?

> (**LORETTA** *reacts.*)

CHORUS GIRL #1. How come she always gets to star in these shows?

CHORUS GIRL #2. She's President of the Drama League. That's why.

(**LORETTA** *doesn't know what to do.*)

Did you see her in the dressing room? She wears bikini underpants. Can you believe it?

(**LORETTA** *screams into the wings.*)

LORETTA. Your body mikes are still on, for God's Sakes!

(*There is a slight pause.*)

CHORUS GIRL #2. (*Off – on mike*) Shit.

SWEET CARNATION'S NAN. Now then. As I was saying. Where is Sweet Carnation? That bloomin' girl. No friends, poor dear. All alone in the world but for me, her old Nan.

(**SWEET CARNATION** *enters from stage left holding flowers and skipping.*)

SWEET CARNATION. Here I am, Nan!

SWEET CARNATION'S NAN. Where were you, in your bloomin' garden?

SWEET CARNATION. Yes, down in the dell. I spent the day sleeping in the flower bed and speaking with my good pals the pansies.

SWEET CARNATION'S NAN. 'ow can flowers be your good pals?

SWEET CARNATION. Easy. They're my good buds.

(*They laugh, thinking the jokes are funny.*)

SWEET CARNATION'S NAN. What do you do down there all day, girl?

SWEET CARNATION. I shoot the breeze.

SWEET CARNATION'S NAN. With 'oo?

SWEET CARNATION. The breeze.

SWEET CARNATION'S NAN Inside with you. I 'ave some news to tell you. News I hope that will cheer your bloomin' 'eart.

SWEET CARNATION. Oh. Can't I sing just one song first?

SWEET CARNATION'S NAN. Okay. But then it's ins-oide witches.

SWEET CARNATION. What?

SWEET CARNATION'S NAN. Inside with you.

SWEET CARNATION. Oh.

> (**SWEET CARNATION'S NAN** *exits into the stage right house.*)

> ### MUSIC CUE #4: "THEY CALL ME SWEET CARNATION"

THEY CALL ME SWEET CARNATION,
BECAUSE I LOVE TO SMELL –
THE FLOWERS IN MY GARDEN,
DOWN THERE IN THE DELL.
I'M ALL ALONE. NO MA. NO PA.
THE BLOOM'S STILL ON MY ROSE.
JUST-MY-BOOK IN BED,
KNOWS HOW-I-LOOK IN BED,
I SLEEP ALONE. IT BLOWS.
MY DREAM IS FOR A GENTLE MAN,
WHO LOVES THE FLOWERS AND SOIL.
HE'LL BE MY KNIGHT IN SHINING BOOTS,
AND I SHALL BE HIS GO-IL.
A GARDEN IS FOR LOVERS' EYES.
THE MOURNING GLORIES KNOW.
HE'LL BE MY SHOVEL STRONG AND TRUE,
AND I SHALL BE HIS HOE.
WE'LL PLANT OUR SEEDS TOGETHER,
AND WATCH OUR COCKLESHELLS,
SOMEDAY I'LL KNOW TRUE BLISS DIVINE,
BUT IN THE MEANTIME, I'LL JUST SMELL...

> *(She curtsy-bows and exits to the house. The*
> **NAUGHTY BOY** *and the* **GIRLS** *re-enter, clog-*
> *dancing.)*

CHORUS GIRL #1. Don't leave us, Naughty Boy.

NAUGHTY BOY. Sorry, girls. The Naughty Boy knows no settling down. Besides, there's only so much of the Naughty Boy to go around.

CHORUS GIRL #2. Oh, please. Just a little more of the old slap and tickle?

NAUGHTY BOY. Tell you what. I'll slap you now. But you'll have to come back later for the tickle.

> *(The* **GIRLS** *cheer. The shutters on the second story*
> *of the stage right house try to open from the inside.*
> *But they are locked from onstage.)*

CHORUS GIRL #3. O Naughty Boy. You make us blush.

NAUGHTY BOY. Don't I know it.

> *(***SWEET CARNATION** *punches her fist through the*
> *window of the stage right house from backstage,*
> *opens the lock, and then the window. She appears*
> *in the window on her balcony.)*

Ah! But who is she who in yonder window sits?

CHORUS GIRL #2. That's Sweet Carnation. The bloom is still on her rose.

> *(The* **CHORUS GIRLS** *giggle and exit.)*

NAUGHTY BOY. Ah, sweet nectar. I would give my life to hear an angel such as she speak but a single word. Oh, how shall I draw her attention? Yes. A pebble. A pebble at her window.

> *(He mimes a pebble toss.)*
>
> *(Sound Effects: "Pebble Hitting Glass")*
>
> *(***SWEET CARNATION** *doesn't hear her cue. She*
> *picks lint off her costume.)*

Perhaps another pebble at her window.

(He mimes a second pebble toss.)

(Sound Effects: "Pebble Hitting Glass")

(She fixes her hair. The **NAUGHTY BOY** *finds a pebble on the stage floor.)*

NAUGHTY BOY. I'll give you a pebble at the window.

(The **NAUGHTY BOY** *throws a real pebble just as* **SWEET CARNATION** *turns to speak. She swallows the pebble and chokes. She spits it out. It rolls off the stage.)*

SWEET CARNATION. Didst someone call?

NAUGHTY BOY. I didst. Sweet maiden. What is thy name?

SWEET CARNATION. They call me Sweet Carnation, because I love to smell.

NAUGHTY BOY. Oh, to sniff your sweet petunias.

SWEET CARNATION. And your name?

NAUGHTY BOY. They call me the Naughty Boy. I have searched for thee the world over...

(making appropriate hand gestures)

...far and wide...

(making a peace sign and miming an afro)

...to and fro. Over Smith & Dale.

SWEET CARNATION. You speak as if you know me, sir.

NAUGHTY BOY. We've never met, yet I know thee. I know thee as I know my own smile. My own breath. My own...

(He blanks. And panics. The composer mouths the line. The **NAUGHTY BOY** *cannot make out* **BERNIE***'s lips. He mouths "what?" the composer mouths it again.)*

My own... "sock drawer?"

SWEET CARNATION. I always dreamed I'd hear those sweet, sweet words. At last! It's you!

NAUGHTY BOY. You know me, sweet maiden?

SWEET CARNATION. Yes. I think I do.

MUSIC CUE #5: "ONCE UPON A TIME"

(The **NAUGHTY BOY** *holds his arms up, outstretched, during the following verse. His arms eventually cramp up and hang lifeless by his side.)*

SWEET CARNATION.
> ONCE UPON A TIME,
> AND VERY LONG AGO,
> SOMEWHERE IN A DREAM,
> WE'VE LOVED BEFORE, I KNOW.
> IN A HEAVENLY GARDEN.
> BEYOND THE MISTS OF TIME,
> YOU HELD ME IN YOUR ARMS,
> AND TOLD ME YOU WERE MINE.
> AND NOW YOU STAND BEFORE ME,
> JUST LIKE MY DREAM COME TRUE.
> TELL ME, MY SWEET STRANGER,
> OH, HAVE YOU DREAMED THIS, TOO?

> *(She loses her balance and falls backwards out of sight.)*

> *(Sound Effects: "Quick Horrible Crash")*

> *(The* **NAUGHTY BOY** *reacts. A moment later,* **SWEET CARNATION** *limps out from the front door of the house. On the second verse, we hear a booming voice come out of the* **NAUGHTY BOY** *as he lip-syncs in an exaggerated way to a [offstage] deep-throated baritone on the offstage mike)*

NAUGHTY BOY.
> AN ANGEL I'D SWEAR WAS YOU,
> STOOD 'NEATH THAT LILAC TREE.
> AND SIGHED WITHIN MY ARMS,
> TO LOVE ETERNALLY.
> FOREVER I'VE BEEN SEARCHING,
> EACH NIGHT A GIRL THAT'S NEW.
> AND AS THEY SLEPT BESIDE ME,
> I ALWAYS DREAMED OF YOU.
> AND NOW MY SEARCH HAS ENDED,

I'M NE'ER TO ROAM AGAIN.
AND WHEN YOU SLEEP BESIDE ME,
I'LL ALWAYS PICTURE THEM.

> *(He twirls her out and in.)*

SWEET CARNATION.

OH, NO! COULD IT BE?
YOU'RE MY DREAM. MY DESTINY.

> *(He twirls her out and lets go. She flies offstage.)*

> *(Sound Effects: "Offstage Crash")*

> *(The* **NAUGHTY BOY** *lip-syncs, but the real singer has been injured by the fall offstage. He coughs and sputters through the solo.)*

NAUGHTY BOY.

AT LAST! WE FINALLY MEET.
AND I MUST END MY SEARCH SO SWEET.

> *(***SWEET CARNATION*** is shoved back out to finish the number.)*

BOTH.

FOR ONCE UPON A TIME,
ONE STARRY NIGHT OF BLUE,
WE DREAMED A DREAM OF LOVE,
AND NOW THAT DREAM COMES TRUE.
OUR DREAM COMES TRUE...

> *(They pose in a dip.* **NAUGHTY BOY** *drops her to take a bow. After the bows, they embrace again.)*

SWEET CARNATION. So help me, I could kiss you.

NAUGHTY BOY. So kiss me, I could help you. I swear from this day forward, you are the only girl for me.

> *(They go to kiss.* **SWEET CARNATION'S NAN** *enters.)*

SWEET CARNATION'S NAN. Wait! Are you bloomin' starkers? Have you lost all sense of yourself? Are you out of your wickety crickety minds? You two can never be together! No way! Never!

SWEET CARNATION. Why not, Nan? The Naughty Boy is my soul and my heart's inspiration. He's all I need to get me by.

CARNATION'S NAN. Let me tell you a lit-tle story, darling. Gather round. Gather 'round everyone.

> ### MUSIC CUE #6: "I'M SWEET CARNATION'S NAN"
>
> *(The* **CHORUS** *skips in and gathers with beer steins, as* **NAN** *sings:)*

SWEET CARNATION'S NAN.

> I'M SWEET CARNATION'S NAN.
> CARNATION'S NAN I AM.
> I LIKES ME TEA, I LIKES ME JAM.
> I'M SWEET CARNATION'S NAN.

> *(Re:* **SWEET CARNATION***)*

> LONG AGO, WHEN SHE WAS JUST A LASS,
> AND I HAD A SLIGHTLY SMALLER ASS,
> GAVE ME ALL, I DID, WAS GOOD AND TRUE.
> TILL I DID WHAT I SHOULDN'TA DO.
> I'M SWEET CARNATION'S NAN.
> CARNATION'S NAN I AM.
> I LIKES TO BELCH,
> WHEN I SCRATCH MESELF.
> I'M SWEET CARNATION'S NAN.
> YES, ME DEAR, I WAS DOWN ON ME LUCK,
> I WAS HUNGRY, DESPERATE FOR A BUCK,
> SAW MAIL-ORDER BRIDES
> BROUGHT LOTS OF GOLD.
> SO I SAID WHAT THE HELL.
> NOW YOUR ASS IS SOLD.

CHORUS.

> SHE'S SWEET CARNATION'S NAN.
> CARNATION'S NAN SHE AM.

SWEET CARNATION'S NAN.

> I COUGH AND SPIT,
> AND IT'S HARD TO SIT.

SWEET CARNATION'S NAN/CHORUS.

I'M (SHE'S) SWEET CARNATION'S NAN.

SWEET CARNATION'S NAN.

YOU'LL GET USED TO IT, DEARIE,
IN DUE TIME.
I'D'A SOLD MESELF,
BUT WHAT'S A DIME?

(to **NAUGHTY BOY***)*

SO YOU SEE WHY SHE CAN'T MARRY YOU.
THE MAJOR-GENERAL'S COMING
AND PAY DAY'S DUE.

CHORUS.

SHE'S SWEET CARNATION'S NAN.
CARNATION'S NAN SHE AM.

SWEET CARNATION'S NAN.

I HAVE CRUST IN ME EYES,
FROM THESE GODDAMN STIES.

CHORUS.

SHE'S SWEET CARNATION'S NAN.

SWEET CARNATION'S NAN.

I HAVE HAIR ON ME CHIN,
AND PUCK-MARKED SKIN,

CHORUS.

SHE'S SWEET CARNATION'S NAN.

SWEET CARNATION'S NAN.

MY TEETH ARE BLACK,
FROM THE PLEGMMY HACK,

CHORUS.

SHE'S SWEET CARNATION'S NAN.

SWEET CARNATION'S NAN.

ME LEGS' GOT VEINS,
FROM ME BIG GAS PAINS,

CHORUS.

SHE'S SWEET CARNATION'S NAN.

SWEET CARNATION'S NAN.

ME BREATH I'D AVOID,
AND I GOT HEMORRHOIDS.

SWEET CARNATION'S NAN/CHORUS.

I'M (SHE'S) SWEET CARNATION'S NAN...!

> (*The number shifts into a wild tap dance number – for no good reason at all.*)

SWEET CARNATION'S NAN. Here she is, boys! Stand back. I'm gonna shake it again. Whoo! Don't want to get any on ya!

> (*The number gets even wilder with* **LORETTA** *spinning crazily around the stage, buck and winging to a climactic finish.*)

CHORUS.

SHE'S SWEET CARNATION'S NAN
CARNATION'S NAN SHE AM

SWEET CARNATION'S NAN.

I'M SWEET...

CHORUS.

SHE'S OH-SO-SWEET CARNATION-IS

SWEET CARNATION'S NAN.

CARNATION'S...

CHORUS.

LOOK OUT FOR HER NAN

SWEET CARNATION'S NAN.

NAN...!

CHORUS.

> (*underneath, as* **NAN** *holds the last note*)

SHE'S THE NAN.
THE NAN SHE AM.
SHE'S SWEET... CARNATION'S... NAN...!

> (**SWEET CARNATION'S NAN** *hocks and spits on the final note. After her bow, the* **CHORUS** *exits and* **SWEET CARNATION'S NAN** *breaks down sobbing.* **SWEET CARNATION** *goes to her.*)

SWEET CARNATION. There, there, Nan. Don't cry. You were only trying to put food on our table.

SWEET CARNATION'S NAN. Then you don't mind?

SWEET CARNATION. Not at all. Even though my life is forever ruined.

SWEET CARNATION'S NAN. Bless ya. Bless ya.

SWEET CARNATION. *(To* **NAUGHTY BOY***)* Well, that does it, then. We can never wed now!

NAUGHTY BOY. Yes. And just as I swore off all other women, too! Darn my timing!

SWEET CARNATION. I guess you can go back to all those other girls.

NAUGHTY BOY. And go against my word? Never! What kind of an Englishman do you think I am? Besides, how could a man be content with mere emeralds after he's seen the emeralds in your eyes? How could a man be content with a moonlit night after he's spent a moonlit night in your embrace? And how could a man be content with the smell of a rose after he's smelled a...

> *(He blanks.* **BERNIE** *the conductor mouths the line. The* **NAUGHTY BOY** *can't make out the words.* **BERNIE** *mouths again.)*

...after he's smelled a...lumbar squat.

> *(***BERNIE** *sits in frustration and reads the program.)*

SWEET CARNATION. Yes. Well, what I think you mean to say is "Isn't there a higher calling."

SWEET CARNATION'S NAN. 'igher than an Englishman's word?

NAUGHTY BOY. You mean... "The Calling of Love?"

> *(The* **CHORUS GIRLS** *immediately enter and pose for a song, holding large paper carnation hearts. No music is played.* **BERNIE** *is lost in reading the program and doesn't hear his cue.)*

You mean... "The Calling of Love?" A higher power being "The Calling of Love?"

> *(giving up)*

But that's not important now, I guess.

(Everyone slinks offstage leaving **SWEET CARNATION'S NAN**, **SWEET CARNATION** *and the* **NAUGHTY BOY**.)*

(The **MAYOR** *and* **THE FOOL** *enter.* **THE FOOL** *enters eating a sandwich, which he then tries to hide.)*

MAYOR. *(Ad libbing, to* **SWEET CARNATION'S NAN**) Out of the way, you big fat yak woman.

LORETTA (NAN). "Yak woman?"

MAYOR. Shut your trap, you toothless cow-faced guttersnipe. Someone's coming. He's dressed as a major-general in the army. Sound the trumpets, Fool.

*(***THE FOOL** *mimes blowing a trumpet, after he hides his sandwich between his legs.)*

(Sound Effects: "Trumpets Fanfare")

Crash the cymbals, Fool!

*(***THE FOOL** *mime crashing cymbals.)*

(Sound Effects: "Cymbals Crash")

(He then goes to eat his sandwich.)

(Ad libbing) Bang the drums, Fool!

*(***THE FOOL** *bites into his sandwich as we hear:)*

(Sound Effects: "Cow Mooing")

*(***THE FOOL** *reacts to his sandwich and puts it away.)*

SWEET CARNATION'S NAN. *(Looking off)* It must be the Major-General.

(To **SWEET CARNATION**)

Your Major-General.

SWEET CARNATION. My husband?

NAUGHTY BOY. My doom.

MAYOR. My my! Do I sense unhappiness in my hamlet?

SWEET CARNATION. Yes. You see, Nan – ever on the lookout for a better life for me – sold me body and soul to a brutish Major-General who will this very day take me as a bride and sexual play thing to do with what he will. In the meantime I've met the Naughty Boy and fallen in love and wish to be wed to he. Our dilemma is simple. Do we keep the bargain my Nan agreed to – which will make me miserable beyond pity – or is there an even higher calling, like "The Calling of Love?"

(*The* CHORUS GIRLS *enter and pose again.*)

(*Hinting to conductor*) "The Calling of Love?"

(BERNIE *is turned away from the stage, cleaning his ear with his finger, and doesn't hear the cue.*)

MAYOR. You mean… "The Calling of Love?"

CHORUS GIRL #1. She means "The Calling of Love."

SWEET CARNATION. Oh, get back in line.

CHORUS GIRL #1. But…

SWEET CARNATION. Ah, forget it.

(*mutters*)

I only have three stinking songs in the whole show…

CHORUS GIRL #1. Three too many if you ask me. We all know why you got the lead. And it wasn't because of your voice.

SWEET CARNATION. Bitch.

(*The* CHORUS *exits.*)

MAYOR. Ya ya. So anyway.

(*To* NAUGHTY BOY)

You're an Englishman. You can never break your word, Naughty Boy.

NAUGHTY BOY. That's what I said.

SWEET CARNATION. O hideous dilemma.

SWEET CARNATION'S NAN. You must help us, Mayor. I'll do anything. Anything.

MAYOR. *(ad libbing)* Then go put a bag over your head and keep me from gagging, you garlic-reeking, bosom drooping old sow.

LORETTA (SWEET CARNATION'S NAN). Stick to the script, Chuck.

MAYOR. *(enjoying himself)* "Stick to the script?" Your breasts are sticking to the floor!

> **(SWEET CARNATION'S NAN** *grabs the back of his tights and pulls. He is castrated.)*

SWEET CARNATION'S NAN. *(to MAYOR)* As I was sayin', if you helps me Sweet Carnation, I promise to focus me attentions on another man. Never to wait for ye. Or bother ye again. I'll just live out me life in a pathetic maiden's squalor.

MAYOR. *(high-pitched)* Deal.

> **(SWEET CARNATION** *&* the **NAUGHTY BOY** *rejoice.)*

SWEET CARNATION. Oh happiness divine!

NAUGHTY BOY. Ditto!

SWEET CARNATION'S NAN. Bless you, sir. Bless you.

NAUGHTY BOY. But wait. How can we do this? I can't break our word. I'm an Englishmen.

CHORUS. *(Entering on cue)* Hooray!

> ### MUSIC CUE #7: "I AM FIRST AN ENGLISHMAN"

NAUGHTY BOY.
> I AM FIRST AN ENGLISHMAN,
> A NOBLE, CULTURED ENGLISHMAN,
> THAT'S WHY MY SHOES ARE SPICK AND SPAN,
> BECAUSE I AM AN ENGLISHMAN.

TOWNSFOLK.
> HE IS FIRST AN ENGLISHMAN,
> A NOBLE, CULTURED ENGLISHMAN,
> THAT'S WHY HIS SHOES ARE SPICK AND SPAN,

ALL.
> BECAUSE HE IS (I AM) AN ENGLISHMAN.

TOWNSFOLK.

> HE MIGHT HAVE BEEN A ROOS-IAN,
> OR EVEN BEEN A PROOS-IAN,
> A TURK OR AN ALBANIAN,
> A SWEDE OR A LON CHANEY-AN,
> A SPANIARD OR PARISIENNE,
> AN ESKIMO ARTESI-AN,

ALL.

> BUT NO (I AM) HE IS AN ENGLISHMAN!

NAUGHTY BOY.

> YES, I AM AN ENGLISHMAN,
> A TIGHT-ASSED LITTLE ENGLISHMAN,
> MY TEETH ARE BAD, I GET NO TAN,
> BECAUSE I AM AN ENGLISHMAN.

TOWNSFOLK.

> YES, HE IS AN ENGLISHMAN,
> A TIGHT-ASSED LITTLE ENGLISHMAN,
> HIS TEETH ARE BAD, HE GETS NO TAN,

ALL.

> BECAUSE HE IS (I AM) AN ENGLISHMAN.

> *(The* **NAUGHTY BOY** *dances and struts during the following.)*

TOWNSFOLK.

> HE ISN'T A SOMAL-I-AN,
> OR EVEN AN I-TAHL-I-AN,
> HE'S NOT A LITHUANIAN,
> HE'S NO BIG FAT UKRAINIAN,
> HE ISN'T FROM AFGHANISTAN,
> HE'S NOT A HEATHEN HINDUSTAN,

ALL.

> BUT NO (I AM) HE IS AN ENGLISHMAN!

NAUGHTY BOY.

> LOOK AT ME, AN ENGLISHMAN,
> A FOPPISH POMPOUS ENGLISHMAN,
> I DRESS IN DRAG, I GOT NO CAN,
> BECAUSE I AM AN ENGLISHMAN.

TOWNSFOLK.

LOOK AT HIM, AN ENGLISHMAN,
A FOPPISH POMPOUS ENGLISHMAN,
HE GETS IN DRAG, HE'S GOT NO CAN,

ALL.

BECAUSE HE IS (I AM) AN ENGLISHMAN.
ROOS-IAN, PROOS-IAN,
ALBANIAN, LON CHANEY-AN,
PARISIENNE, ARTESI-AN,
SOMAL-I-AN, I-TAHL-I-AN,
LITH-WAN-I-AN, UKRAINIAN,
AFGHANISTAN, A HINDUSTAN,
BUT NO (I AM) HE IS AN ENGLISHMAN!

NAUGHTY BOY.

I'M A STINKING ENGLISHMAN,
A PANTY-WEARING ENGLISHMAN,
I SLEEP WITH SHEEP ON THE DIVAN,
BECAUSE I AM AN ENGLISHMAN.

TOWNSFOLK.

HE'S A STINKING ENGLISHMAN,
A PANTY-WEARING ENGLISHMAN,
HE SLEEPS WITH SHEEP ON THE DI-VAN,

ALL.

BECAUSE HE IS (I AM) AN ENGLISHMAN.
(I AM) HE'S FIRST AN ENG-LISH-MAN...!

(The **CHORUS** *exits.)*

NAUGHTY BOY. So, you see, Sweet Carnation, we're sunk!

SWEET CARNATION. Damn your being English.

MAYOR. Wait. Holy Mackerel. I just remembered. I can break my word.

NAUGHTY BOY. How?

SWEET CARNATION. Yes, how?

SWEET CARNATION'S NAN. Yes, 'ow?

MICKEY (NAUGHTY BOY). *(Concerned)* What's the matter?

LORETTA (SWEET CARNATION'S NAN). Nothing.

NAUGHTY BOY. Oh.

(to **MAYOR***)*

How can you break your word, Mayor?

MAYOR. Easy. I'm not English. I live in the Alps.

NAUGHTY BOY. By Jove. He's right.

SWEET CARNATION'S NAN. 'e's so brainy, 'e is.

MAYOR. And so sure am I that I can make everyone in my hamlet happy this very day, that I vow here and now to marry you, old toothless odor-reeking Nan, should I fail in this my given task.

SWEET CARNATION'S NAN. O anticipated rapture! You're a witness! You're a witness!

NAUGHTY BOY. What shall we do, Mayor?

MAYOR. First things first. Run and hide. The Major-General approaches.

SWEET CARNATION. How do you know?

MAYOR. Women are swooning.

(Sound Efects: "Women Swoon.")

Trumpets are sounding.

(Sound Effects: "Trumpets Fanfare.")

And he's standing right over there.

(spotlight on the **MAJOR-GENERAL** *– in a kaiser WWI uniform)*

*(***SWEET CARNATION** *and* **NAUGHTY BOY** *exit stage left.)*

MUSIC CUE #8: "I AM A SOLDIER"

(The women squeal as the **MAJOR-GENERAL** *marches in all his splendor. The* **TOWNSFOLK** *all march along, turning the song into an elaborate pinwheel number.)*

MAJOR-GENERAL.

I AM A SOLDIER,
I'M BRAVE AND TRUE.
AND I BEAT THE CRAP,

OUT OF MEN LIKE YOU.
I SLASH THEIR CHESTS,
AND I GOUGE THEIR EYES,
AND I TAKE WHAT'S LEFT,
AND I MAKE MEAT PIES.

CHORUS.

HE'S BRAVE AND TRUE
BEATS MEN LIKE YOU.
SO HIDE YOUR EYES.
OR HE'LL MAKE MEAT PIES.

MAJOR-GENERAL.

THEN I GRAB THEIR HAIR,
AND WHACK OFF THEIR HEAD,
THEN I KICK IT AROUND,
TO MAKE SURE IT'S DEAD.
AND I STICK THE SKULL,
ON A BIG LONG SPIKE.
AND I MARCH AROUND,
AND I CALL IT "MIKE."

CHORUS.

BLEED FROM THE HEAD,
YOU'LL BE QUITE DEAD.
YOUR HEAD ON-A SPIKE,
WITH-A NEW NAME "MIKE."

MAJOR-GENERAL.

FOR I'M A SOLDIER,
BRAVE AND TRUE.
AND I'LL RAPE YOUR WIFE,
AND I'LL RAPE YOU, TOO.
I'LL CUT OUT YOUR HEART,
LIKE A PIECE OF SPAM,
NOW I'M SORRY FOLKS,
THAT'S THE WAY I AM.

CHORUS.

HE'S BRAVE AND TRUE,
HE'LL RAPE YOU, TOO.
HE EATS HIS SPAM,
THAT'S THE WAY HE AM.

MAJOR-GENERAL/CHORUS.
  THAT'S THE KIND OF GUY I (HE) AM!

MAYOR. *(His arm resting on* **THE FOOL***'s shoulder)* Major-General, I am the Mayor of Himm.

MAJOR-GENERAL. *(Confused, pointing to* **THE FOOL***)* You're his mayor?

MAYOR. Of course. I am everyone's mayor.

MAJOR-GENERAL. Then why say you are just the mayor of that fellow?

MAYOR. I didn't.

MAJOR-GENERAL. You did.

MAYOR. I didn't. I said I was the mayor of Himm.

MAJOR-GENERAL. I know. But what about them?

MAYOR. What about them?

MAJOR-GENERAL. Who is their mayor?

MAYOR. That is me, as well. I am the mayor of Himm.

MAJOR-GENERAL. Yes. You keep saying that. But what about them?

MAYOR. What about them?

MAJOR-GENERAL. Who is their mayor?

MAYOR. That would be me.

MAJOR-GENERAL. Then say it, man.

MAYOR. I am the Mayor of Himm.

MAJOR-GENERAL. And them.

MAYOR. Of course!

MAJOR-GENERAL. So you are the mayor of everybody.

MAYOR. No, that would be my cousin, Egbert. He's the Mayor of Everybody. I am merely the Mayor of Himm.

MAJOR-GENERAL. But what about them?

MAYOR. What about them?

MAJOR-GENERAL. Are you their mayor as well?

MAYOR. Of course. I am the Mayor of Himm.

MAJOR-GENERAL. And them?

MAYOR. Of course. I am everyone's mayor.

MAJOR-GENERAL. But not the Mayor of Everybody.

MAYOR. That is the truth.

MAJOR-GENERAL. So let me get this straight. You are the mayor of Himm, and the mayor of them. And although you're everyone's mayor, you're not the Mayor of Everybody.

MAYOR. Exactly.

MAJOR-GENERAL. I don't even know what I'm talking about!

> *(The* **MAYOR** *and the* **MAJOR-GENERAL** *bow after their version of a classic "who's on first?" routine. The other cast members applaud them.)*

I am looking for Sweet Carnation's Nan. I have paid a great deal of money for the hand of Sweet Carnation.

THE FOOL. You paid money for her hand? And they call me a fool.

MAYOR. Quiet, Fool.

SWEET CARNATION'S NAN. I am Sweet Carnation's Nan.

MAJOR-GENERAL. Good God, woman. I'll strike you dead if there is even the slightest resemblance between your hideous hide and the angel I call my own.

SWEET CARNATION'S NAN. Oh, Mr. Lah-dee-dah. Awful full of yourself, now, aren't you? And what if little Sweet Carnation doesn't think you're so sportin'?

MAYOR. Quiet, you bow-legged pigeon-breasted whiff of a mule. Have no fear, Major-General. She is not Sweet Carnation's mother. They're not even related. Sweet Carnation's parents were washed overboard in a tragic boating mishap.

SWEET CARNATION'S NAN. Yes. They was out in their lit-tle dingy-boat when a giant wave washed them over the side. Me? I was sit-ting on me dock a fishing for me supper when I heard the horrible screams. I looked up and there they was, a coughing, and a spittin' and a bobbin' in the briny. And then they was no more. Next thing I knows, I feel a tug on me line. And right on the end of me hook, I reels in a lit-tle baby.

And as I smelled the fish-scented air, and looked at the lit-tle fishy-smellin' orphan hangin' next to the big stinkin' fish on me hook, I says to meself: "I shall name her Sweet Carnation." And I raised the lit-tle nipper as my own ever since.

MAJOR-GENERAL. *(Smacking her hard on the back)* What a sainted fisherwoman you are. I cannot thank you enough for saving my beloved angel. Now tell me where she is before I break your wart-encrusted neck.

MAYOR. It seems there has been a slight delay in presenting you your mail-order bride.

MAJOR-GENERAL. Why is there a delay with my mail-order bride?

MAYOR. Well, you know how slow the mail is.

(They acknowledge their punch-line.)

…Anyway.

MAJOR-GENERAL. Look, a man has needs. And a man my size has extra large needs.

(The women swoon.)

If she is not here in but a moment, I'll kill you and everyone in this hamlet.

(Everyone gasps.)

And now if you'll excuse me, I shall go plunder and rape your entire village.

(The crowd cheers.)

SWEET CARNATION'S NAN. *(Pointing to stage right house)* I live over here.

MAJOR-GENERAL. *(Pointing off left)* Then I'll start over there.

(He exits.)

MAYOR. Quick, old toothless large-footed girl. Shake your big fat can and find me Sweet Carnation and the Naughty Boy. We'll disguise them as other peoples.

LORETTA. *(Sotto, turning her back on the audience)* There's nothing in the script about a big fat can.

MAYOR. Away, foul-smelling hag woman!
Let me think. What to do? What to do?

MUSIC CUE #9: "A PLAN, A SCHEME"

A PLAN! A SCHEME!
WHAT CAN MY MIND DEVISE?
A RISK! A DARE!
COULD THIS PROVE TO BE UNWISE?
A RUSE! A PLOT!
I'VE GOT IT! A DISGUISE!

(Spying the town fool bending over some flowers)

BUT HOW? BUT WHO?
WHY IT'S RIGHT HERE BEFORE MY EYES!
IT'S YOU! IT'S TRUE!
YOU'LL SIMPLY HAVE TO FEMINIZE!

THE FOOL.

IT'S ME? IT'S I?
I DON'T QUITE UNDERSTAND-ER-SIZE.

MAYOR.

OH YES! IT'S YOU!
YOU'LL BE A GIRL BEFORE HIS EYES!

THE FOOL.

OH ME. OH MY!
I CAN'T. I MUST APOLOGIZE!

MAYOR.

OH, YES! YOU WILL!
OR ELSE I'LL HAVE TO MURDER-IZE.

THE FOOL.

OKAY! ALL RIGHT!
I GUESS I'LL HAVE TO COMPROMISE!

MAYOR. *(With **THE FOOL** in a head-lock)*
OH YES! OH TRUE!
BUT FIRST YOU MUST DEODORIZE!

THE FOOL. *(Getting into the idea)*
AND THEN! AND WHEN
DO WE BEGIN TO GLAMOR-IZE?

MAYOR. *(Dragging* **THE FOOL** *off)*
ENOUGH! ENOUGH!
OR I WILL START TO CIRCUMCISE!

THE FOOL. *(As they exit to house stage right)*
OH HEART! OH NERVES!
I HOPE I DO NOT FERTILIZE!

TOWNSFOLK.
IT'S TRUE! IT'S TRUE!
IT'S TRUE! IT'S TRUE! IT'S TRUE!
HE'S GOING TO BE FEMINIZED.
HE HOPES HE DOES NOT FERTILIZE.
NOT FERTILIZE. NOT FERTILIZE.
AT FIRST HE'LL BE DEODORIZED
AND THEN HE'LL BE IMMORTALIZED.
FIRST GLAMORIZED. THEN FEMINIZED.
DEODORIZED. BEFORE HIS EYES.

> *(The* **GIRLS** *dance the french can-can. On their second move forward, the* **GIRLS** *are joined in the* **CHORUS** *line by a sixth girl – the town fool who is now in drag, dressed like a village girl.)*

HE'S GLAMORIZED. AND FEMINIZED.
DEODORIZED. BEFORE OUR EYES.
FIRST HE WAS DEODORIZED,
AND NOW HE IS IMMORTALIZED.
AND RIGHT BEFORE OUR EYES...!

> *(The* **MAJOR-GENERAL** *enters.)*

MAJOR-GENERAL. Well, where is she?

MAYOR. Allow me to present the sweetest thing on earth.

> *(The* **SERGEANT** *enters with his* **PATROLMEN** *from backstage, pre-occupied with finding the escapee, unaware he's onstage.)*

SERGEANT. Well, he's not back here.

> *(The actors freeze.)*

MAYOR. Get off.

SERGEANT. Oh. I didn't realize this was the...sorry.

(The **PATROLMEN** *laugh at the SERGEANT as they exit quickly backstage.)*

(SWEET CARNATION'S NAN *enters, pushing on* **THE FOOL.** *)*

SWEET CARNATION'S NAN. 'ere she is.

MAJOR-GENERAL. *(Eying* **THE FOOL** *)* O Sweet rapture! Never have I seen such beauty.

(THE FOOL *looks behind him to see who he's talking to. The* **MAYOR** *and* **SWEET CARNATION'S NAN** *exit.)*

That oh so feminine face. That lush womanly figure. Those meaty girlish hands. You're all women and all women are you.

THE FOOL. I'm not like other girls.

MAJOR-GENERAL. I'll say. You are the woman I've always dreamed about.

MUSIC CUE #10: "ONCE UPON A TIME" – REPRISE

ONCE UPON A TIME,
AND VERY LONG AGO,
SOMEWHERE IN A DREAM,
WE'VE LOVED BEFORE, I KNOW.
IN A HEAVENLY GARDEN,
BEYOND THE MISTS OF TIME,
YOU HELD ME IN YOUR ARMS,
AND TOLD ME YOU WERE MINE.
AND NOW YOU STAND BEFORE ME,
JUST LIKE MY DREAM COME TRUE.
TELL ME, MY SWEET STRANGER,
OH, HAVE YOU DREAMED THIS, TOO?

THE FOOL.

MY DREAM'S A LITTLE DIFFERENT,
BUT GEE, YOUR DREAM SEEMS SWELL.
AND FOR MY WEDDING NIGHT,
I'LL PROB'LY BURN IN HELL.
THE CLOUDS ABOVE ARE RAINFUL,

BUT SUN WILL SOON BURST THROUGH.

(*Eying the* **MAJOR**)

MY GOD, THIS COULD BE PAINFUL,
BUT WHAT AM I TO DO?
BE GENTLE WITH ME DARLING,
I'M VERY SMALL IN SIZE.
TONIGHT WHEN WE BECOME ONE,
YOU'RE IN FOR A SURPRISE.

MAJOR-GENERAL.

OH, YES! COULD IT BE?
YOU'RE MY DREAM. MY DESTINY.

(*He puckers.* **THE FOOL** *freaks out.*)

THE FOOL.

OY GOD! HE WANTS A KISS.

(*Covering his mouth*)

JESUS CHRIST, MY ORIFICE.

BOTH.

FOR ONCE UPON A TIME,
ONE STARRY NIGHT OF BLUE
WE DREAMED A DREAM OF LOVE,
AND NOW THAT DREAM COMES TRUE.
OUR DREAM COMES TRUE.

(*The* **MAJOR-GENERAL** *goes to kiss* **THE FOOL.**)

THE FOOL. Wait! You're going to kiss me before all these people?

MAJOR-GENERAL. Yes. They can kiss you afterward.

THE FOOL. Wait! Shouldn't we be singing and dancing?

MAJOR-GENERAL. Why?

THE FOOL. There's going to be a wedding!

(*The people cheer. The music starts.* **THE FOOL** *escapes from his embrace as everyone dances and sings.*)

MUSIC CUE #11: "THERE'S GOING TO BE A WEDDING"

ALL.

> THERE'S GOING TO BE A WEDDING.
> A WEDDING. A WEDDING.
> THERE'S GOING TO BE A WEDDING,
> AND TODAY'S THE DAY.
> IN CASE YOU WERE FORGETTING.
> FORGETTING. THE WEDDING.
> THERE'S GOING TO BE A WEDDING.

> > *(As* **THE FOOL** *enters with a bouquet)*

> WHAT A NICE BOUQUET!
> THERE'S GOING TO BE A WEDDING,
> AND TODAY'S THE DAY!

> > *(Everyone cheers. The* **MAJOR-GENERAL** *goes to kiss* **THE FOOL.** **THE FOOL** *ducks under his arms and escapes in the crowd.)*

MAJOR-GENERAL. Come back here, minx.

> > *(The* **MAJOR-GENERAL** *chases* **THE FOOL** *off. The* **MAYOR** *enters.* **SWEET CARNATION** *and* **NAUGHTY BOY** *clog-dance on with* **SWEET CARNATION'S NAN.***)*

SWEET CARNATION'S NAN. Here they are, Mayor. I found them in the garden soiling themselves.

SWEET CARNATION. What shall we do now? Have you got a plan?

MAYOR. Do I?! Get a load of this. I dressed the Fool to look like you and the Major-General fell for it. So I'll perform a double ceremony. I'll marry you two, and at the same time I'll marry the Major-General to the Fool. And when the Major-General finds out who his bride really is, then the joke'll be on him. Because in the Catholic religion, you're married for life!

> > *(Thumbing towards* **LORETTA***)*

> Be-lieve me!

NAUGHTY BOY. But, I say, everyone in the hamlet knows I'm the Naughty Boy. I'm a world famous bon vivant.

MAYOR. What if I disguise you as a different peoples?

NAUGHTY BOY. But who?

> (*Two* **CHORUS BOYS** *enter. One has a big clip-on mustache. The other just happens to have a real mustache.*)

MAYOR. Here. Wear this clever disguise.

> (*The* **MAYOR** *rips the real mustache off* **CHORUS BOY #1.**)

CHORUS BOY #1. Ow…

MAYOR. I mean this clever disguise.

> (*He pulls off the fake mustache off* **CHORUS BOY #2.**)

CHORUS BOY #1. Christ… I'm bleeding.

> (*The* **CHORUS BOYS** *exit.*)

SWEET CARNATION. (*As her bosom heaves*) Oh, Naughty Boy, we're to be married this very day. Be still my heaving bosom.

NAUGHTY BOY. Oh, leave it alone. It's doing just fine.

> (*The* **MAJOR-GENERAL** *and* **THE FOOL** *run on. The* **MAJOR-GENERAL** *wipes his mouth.*)

MAJOR-GENERAL. What a woman!

> (**THE FOOL** *brushes his teeth and spits in disgust.*)

THE FOOL. Scotch. I need scotch.

MAJOR-GENERAL. Begin the ceremony, Mayor, before I smite you down with all my smite. I cannot be delayed another moment from burying myself in the luscious peaches of my bride.

THE FOOL. I can't help it if I'm old-fashioned.

> (*To other* **GIRLS,** *coy*)

They'll never buy the cow if you give the milk for free, you know.

MAYOR. Gather around, everyone!

> (*Everyone gathers.*)

MAYOR. As mayor of the Hamlet of Himm. I announce reason for great rejoicing. There shall be a double ceremony in the land!

(*Everyone cheers.*)

In addition to the Major-General and Sweet Carnation, we're going to marry the Man in the Mustache and That Other Girl!

(*Everyone cheers.*)

CHORUS GIRL. There's going to be two weddings!

(*Everyone cheers.*)

MUSIC CUE #12: "THERE'S GOING TO BE TWO WEDDINGS"

(*Everyone dances and sings.*)

ALL.

THERE'S GOING TO BE TWO WEDDINGS.
TWO WEDDINGS. TWO WEDDINGS.
THERE'S GOING TO BE TWO WEDDINGS,
AND TODAY'S THE DAY.
IN CASE YOU WERE FORGETTING.
FORGETTING. THE WEDDINGS.
THERE'S GOING TO BE TWO WEDDINGS.

(**SWEET CARNATION'S NAN** *enters from her house with a souffle.*)

AND A NICE SOUFFLE!
THERE'S GOING TO BE TWO WEDDINGS,
AND TODAY'S THE DAY!

(*After the bows, we see another man has wandered onstage. He wears black pants, a loose strait-jacket, has a mustache and looks deranged. A beat as everyone reacts.*)

(*It's* **JACKIE BALDO**, *escapee from the home for the criminally insane.*)

CHUCK (MAYOR). (*sotto*) Who the hell is that?

(LORETTA [SWEET CARNATION'S NAN] pulls out the flyer with the photo of JACKIE BALDO and holds it up, realizing:)

LORETTA (SWEET CARNATION'S NAN). Omigod. It's Jackie Baldo.

CHUCK (MAYOR). Who?

LORETTA (SWEET CARNATION'S NAN). From the Home for the Criminally Insane!

(Everyone panics and shrieks.)

CHUCK (MAYOR). *(To JACKIE BALDO, as he pushes LORETTA forward)* Whatever you do, sir, don't rape and kill my wife.

(Everyone panics and shrieks. The SERGEANT enters, gun drawn.)

SERGEANT. Hold it right there, son.

(JACKIE BALDO jumps off the stage and runs down the aisle.)

Get a light on him!

(A spotlight follows JACKIE BALDO as he escapes through a row of seats. The cops follow.)

JACKIE BALDO. Excuse me. Excuse me. Excuse me.

SERGEANT. Excuse me. Excuse me. Excuse me.

(JACKIE BALDO and the SERGEANT exit.)

COREY (SWEET CARNATION). God, I'm so afraid.

BROCK (MAJOR-GENERAL). Don't worry, Sweet Carnation. I'm here.

(The MAJOR-GENERAL (BROCK) realizes he is holding THE FOOL (PETEY). He quickly moves to hold SWEET CARNATION (COREY). Then BROCK turns back to PETEY.)

(to THE FOOL) Have you been working out?

(The actors onstage slowly realize the audience is staring back at them.)

MICKEY (NAUGHTY BOY). Uh...now what?

BERNIE. Stay in character.

SWEET CARNATION'S NAN. Ow, 'oo was that strange man, Mayor?

MAYOR. *(at a loss, giving her a look that can kill)* Uh...a tourist?

> *(A beat, then the entire cast agrees "good answer, good answer.")*
>
> *(going with it)*

You know how popular our hamlet is. Come again, buddy! And don't forget your Visa, 'cause we don't take American Express!

MICKEY (NAUGHTY BOY). Nobody knows what the hell you're talking about, Chuck.

SWEET CARNATION'S NAN. You must be bloomin' starkers. Out of your wickety-crickety mind.

MAYOR. Shut your cakehole, you big-rumped, onion-reeking, haircut of a man.

> *(Back into the show)*

And now...on with the weddings!

MICKEY (NAUGHTY BOY). But what about...

MAYOR. Don't worry, Naughty Boy. Everything will work out all right in the end.

COREY (SWEET CARNATION). How do you know?

MAYOR. This is an operetta.

> *(Everyone cheers.)*

MUSIC CUE #13: "ALWAYS SEE IT THROUGH"

ALWAYS SEE IT THROUGH UNTIL THE END,
IF YOU DON'T KNOW HOW THEN JUST PRETEND.

SWEET CARNATION'S NAN.

THERE'S NO GREATER MESSAGE THAT WE CAN SEND.

BOTH.

> THEN JUST TO SEE IT THROUGH
> TILL THE END.

MAJOR-GENERAL.

> DON'T RETREAT.
> JUST MARCH ON AND DEFEND.
> SHOW YOUR STUFF.
> AND DO WHAT YOU INTEND.

THE FOOL.

> JUST BE CAREFUL WHEN AND WHERE YOU BEND.

MAJOR-GENERAL & THE FOOL.

> AND ALWAYS SEE IT THROUGH TILL THE END.

SWEET CARNATION.

> ANY HEART THAT'S BROKEN YOU CAN MEND.
> JUST BELIEVE IN LO-OVE.

NAUGHTY BOY.

> ALL THE GIRLS I SLEPT WITH
> WERE JUST FRIENDS.

CHORUS GIRLS.

> ROTTEN BASTARD SCHMUCK.

SWEET CARNATION. *(To the **NAUGHTY BOY**)*

> IF THE MAJOR GETS ME IN THE END.
> I'LL JUST CLOSE MY EYES AND JUST PRETEND.
> BUT ONCE I'M IN HEAVEN.
> I'LL BE UP FOR GRABS AGAIN.

ALL.

> JUST TRY TO SEE IT THROUGH TILL THE END.
> ALWAYS SEE IT THOUGH UNTIL THE END,
> IF YOU DON'T KNOW HOW THEN JUST PRETEND.
> THERE'S NO GREATER MESSAGE THAT WE CAN SEND.
> THEN JUST TO SEE IT THROUGH
> TILL THE END.
>
> > *(The older lady **CHORUS GIRL** waves a "Hamlet of Himm" flag.)*
>
> TEY TA RA. BOOM. LA DEE DA DEE DEND.
> TEY TA RA. BOOM. LA DEE DA DEE DEND.
> LA DEE DA. LET'S SING IT ONCE AGAIN.
> ALWAYS SEE IT THROUGH TILL THE END.

(**JACKIE BALDO** *runs on, followed by the cops. All freeze when they see the audience – in their running positions. They turn them into trenches, and dance out the rest of the number.*)

ALL. *(cont.)*

TEY TA RA. BOOM. LA DEE DA DEE DEND.
TEY TA RA. BOOM. LA DEE DA DEE DEND.
ONE LAST TIME, IT'S WHAT WE RECOMMEND.
AND ALWAYS SEE IT THROUGH
ALWAYS SEE IT THROUGH
ALWAYS SEE IT THROUGH TILL THE END

(**JACKIE BALDO** *and the cops take off into the wings.*)

ALWAYS SEE IT THROUGH TILL THE END
ALWAYS SEE IT THROUGH TILL THE END

(*As the final notes are sung, the curtain closes, knocking into the* **CHORUS GIRL** *from the opening bit, along with* **CHORUS BOY #1**. *They fall on their butts in front of the closed curtain. The* **BOY** *quickly rises, stepping on the* **GIRL**'*s skirt as he helps her up, which tears her clothes off yet again. They grab the skirt and scamper offstage.*)

End of Act One

ACT TWO

(Lights: houselights down)

(A spotlight hits **LORETTA PEAMAN** *as she enters to make a curtain speech, still in her costume.)*

LORETTA. Hello. I'm not Sweet Carnation's Nan right now. It's me, Loretta Peaman again.

(After she bows.)

I know you've all seen the policemen scouring the grounds looking for that escaped lunatic Jackie Baldo – who it seems is still at large, but in true show business tradition we have decided the show must go on! So please ignore Sergeant Taggert and his men if they should frisk you or interrogate you at any time during the second act. They are only doing their duty. And now...on with the show!

*(***LORETTA*** has trouble finding the break in the curtain to exit. She ends up crawling underneath. A spotlight appears on* **BERNIE LUDLOE** *as he enters from the wings stage left he starts to take a step down the stairs, stops and glares at the spotlight operator to follow him down the stairs. The light follows him obediently. Once at his conductor's chair,* **BERNIE** *sits. The chair collapses and* **BERNIE** *crashes to the floor. He rises, pulls out a folding chair, sits again, and turns on the iPhone player.)*

MUSIC CUE #14: "ACT TWO ENTR'ACTE"

(The overture plays. During the overture, **JACKIE BALDO** *sneaks through the audience and eventually hides backstage. The* **PATROLMEN**

enter with police dogs and flashlights. They follow through and exit backstage. Finally, the curtain opens to reveal the lead actors in their act one finale positions.)

MUSIC CUE #15: "THERE'S GOING TO BE TWO WEDDINGS"

*(The **CHORUS** dances on with their maypole.)*

ALL.

THERE'S GOING TO BE TWO WEDDINGS,
TWO WEDDINGS. TWO WEDDINGS.
THERE'S GOING TO BE TWO WEDDINGS,
AND TODAY'S THE DAY.
IN CASE YOU WERE FORGETTING.
FORGETTING. THE WEDDINGS.
THERE'S GOING TO BE TWO WEDDINGS.

*(**LORETTA** pulls **CHUCK**'s wig off.)*

SWEET CARNATION'S NAN.

HE'LL WEAR HIS TOUPEE.

CHUCK (MAYOR). *(as he scrambles to put his hair back on:)* Hey!

ALL.

THERE'S GOING TO BE TWO WEDDINGS,
AND TODAY'S THE DAY.

MAYOR. I shall now read the ceremony.

(no prop)

From my mind.

"Dearly beloved, we are gathered here in the happy hamlet of Himm to perform the ever-binding ceremony of Holy Matrimony between the Major-General and Sweet Carnation… As well as between the Man in the Mustache and That Other Girl."

*(As the crowd cheers, the **NAUGHTY BOY** is clubbed in the back of the head and dragged backstage by **JACKIE BALDO**. No one notices.)*

If there be anyone who knows of a reason that these peoples shall not be wed, let him speak now or forever hold his peace.

THE FOOL. *(coyly, to* **MAJOR-GENERAL***)* I'd speak up, but I'm a girl. I don't have a piece.

MAYOR. Repeat after me...

> *(He goes to read, and clears his throat. The others repeat after him.)*

Not that.

ALL. "Not that."

MAYOR. No.

ALL. "No."

MAYOR. Don't repeat that.

ALL. "Don't repeat that."

MAYOR. Stop it.

ALL. "Stop it."

MAYOR. Are you out of your minds?

ALL. "Are you out of your minds?"

MAYOR. Shut up.

ALL. "Shut up."

MAYOR. No more repeating!

> *(silence)*

THE FOOL. No more repeating.

MAYOR. *(smacking the back of* **THE FOOL***'s head, sending his wig flying)* Quiet, Fool.

> *(Broadly, over-acted)*

Oh, no! What have I done?

> *(Everyone gasps.)*

THE FOOL. My hair!

MAJOR-GENERAL. My God!

SWEET CARNATION'S NAN. Mylanta!

MAJOR-GENERAL. What is this? You're no woman!

THE FOOL. I'm more of a woman than you'll ever be.

MAJOR-GENERAL. You're a man!

THE FOOL. No!

> *(looks down dress)*

My God, it's true! Mother why did you lie to me all these years!

MAJOR-GENERAL. That tears it!

> *(The **MAJOR-GENERAL** reaches to draw his sword, and accidentally rips off the skirt of the **CHORUS GIRL**. She runs off. **THE FOOL** cowers.)*

(sword held to nan's throat) Where is the real Sweet Carnation? Speak old woman before you die like a dog.

SWEET CARNATION'S NAN. You mean put to sleep by a family veterinarian?

MAJOR-GENERAL. No. Murdered!

> *(The **SERGEANT** appears in the window of the stage right house. The **PATROLMEN** enter from backstage. **JACKIE BALDO** hides his face.)*

SERGEANT. What was that?

> *(The actors freeze.)*

CHUCK (MAYOR). *(Sotto, embarrassed)* Nothing. Get off the stage.

SERGEANT. *(Sotto, frozen, embarrassed)* I heard "murder."

CHUCK (MAYOR). *(Sotto)* Get off!

SERGEANT. Sorry. I was just…

ALL. Get out of here!

SERGEANT. Right.

> *(The **SERGEANT** slowly sinks out of view.)*

MAJOR-GENERAL. Prepare for the worst, Hamlet of Himm. For deceiving me, you shall all be whipped…

> *(All react with "oohs.")*

Raped…

> *(All react with "aahs.")*

Tortured…

(All react with "oohs.")

And sold into slavery.

(All react with "aahs" – except for **CHORUS BOY #2**.*)*

CHORUS BOY #2. *(Gleefully)* Yes!

SWEET CARNATION'S NAN. Will that be before or after the whipping and the raping?

MAJOR-GENERAL. As for you, Mayor. I shall sever your head and stick my sword down your open neck to disembowel you through your gaping wound and then as I serve your entrails to your dog, I shall laugh at your entire situation!

MAYOR. Then the laugh shall be on you. I don't have a dog!

(Sound Effects: "Dogs Bark Offstage")

(The police run on with the dogs chasing after what appears to be **JACKIE BALDO**, *but is in fact,* **MICKEY** *(The* **NAUGHTY BOY***), gagged, and tied into johnny's strait-jacket. He escapes stage left. The* **PATROLMEN** *exit stage left)*

MAJOR-GENERAL. And…and…and only then after your brutal evisceration shall I search every woman in the hamlet until I find the real Sweet Carnation.

SWEET CARNATION. Wait, Major-General. How will you know the real Sweet Carnation when you find her?

MAJOR-GENERAL. Surely she must have some identifying mark that will distinguish her from the others.

SWEET CARNATION'S NAN. You mean you know about the birthmark on her bum in the shape of Piccadilly Circus?

MAJOR-GENERAL. I do now!

*(*JACKIE BALDO *enters from backstage wearing the* NAUGHTY BOY*'s costume. Unnoticed he takes his place near* SWEET CARNATION.*)*

SWEET CARNATION'S NAN. Ow, me and me big blowhole.

MAYOR. I'm not touching that line with a ten foot steckenbleiben.

SWEET CARNATION. Oh dastardly day of doom. What shall we do, Naughty Boy?

JACKIE BALDO. I just want to use a bathroom with a door on it.

(Silence as everyone turns to see him.)

COREY (SWEET CARNATION). What? Ah!

JACKIE BALDO. Hi, Corey. Do you know how lonely a padded cell can be? When all they give you to keep you going is the entertainment section of old newpapers. By the way, you looked really cute as Annie in that little red dress.

COREY (SWEET CARNATION). *(Choked with fear)* Thank you.

JACKIE BALDO. But clippings aren't enough. You can't smell clippings. Well, you can, but they smell like newspaper...

(In little groups, the entire cast starts to exit, leaving the MAYOR and JACKIE BALDO behind.)

BERNIE. Wait. Don't leave the stage.

(Sotto)

Do something, Chuck.

MAYOR. ...I still don't have a dog!

(Sound Effects: "Dogs Bark Offstage")

(As the PATROLMEN and the police dogs enter stage left JACKIE BALDO runs off stage right the MAYOR runs off upstage left a beat of silence onstage.)

(The NAUGHTY BOY, dressed in JACKIE BALDO's black pants, boots, strait jacket, and gag enters in a daze. Fog begins to cover the stage.)

(Fog effect)

MUSIC CUE #16: "LORD OF THE HAMLET"

(Mysterious celtic music begins to play, and as the **NAUGHTY BOY** *struggles to get out of the strait jacket, the remainder of the cast enters dancing in lines behind him. As they circle him, the* **NAUGHTY BOY** *throws off his strait jacket, and pushes up his gag – which turns into a head band. The number goes on. A black-caped* **SWEET CARNATION** *dances with the* **NAUGHTY BOY***. The number builds to a crescendo, ending with a bare-chested* **NAUGHTY BOY**'s *arms outstretched towards the heavens.* **SWEET CARNATION** *responds with sexual interest. During the applause the* **CHORUS GIRLS** *swarm and eye* **MICKEY** *[The* **NAUGHTY BOY***] with a new respect. They squeeze his arm and wink and smile as they dance past him to exit, leaving* **SWEET CARNATION** *and the* **NAUGHTY BOY** *alone onstage.)*

COREY (SWEET CARNATION). I love the way you look in his pants.

MICKEY (NAUGHTY BOY). I didn't look in his pants.

COREY (SWEET CARNATION). Never mind.

(in character)

Well...what now, Naughty Boy? It's only a matter of time before the Major-General sees the birthmark shaped like Piccadilly Circus on me bum.

NAUGHTY BOY. I say, does it really look like Piccadilly Circus – with the statue and everything?

SWEET CARNATION. Yes, it even has that little fish and chips place you love so much.

NAUGHTY BOY. Really? Oh, dash it all, man! I'd so like to see it.

SWEET CARNATION. But you can't. My bum is connected to the rest of me and the rest of me is promised to the Major-General. But remember this...whether he's touching it, slapping it, or biting it, my heart will always belong to you.

NAUGHTY BOY. You sure he wouldn't want your heart? Cause… I'd be happy to switch parts with him, you know.

SWEET CARNATION. 'Fraid not.

NAUGHTY BOY. Crumpets.

SWEET CARNATION. Maybe you can appeal to his sense of decency.

NAUGHTY BOY. But of course. Maybe, like me, and all other men from England, he'll understand that there is a higher calling.

SWEET CARNATION. You mean… "The Calling of Love?"

> (The **CHORUS** enters, taking their place. **BERNIE LUDLOE**, cocky now, presses play on the iPhone player.)

MUSIC CUE #17: "THE CALLING OF LOVE"

> (A music intro plays. The **NAUGHTY BOY** sings:)

NAUGHTY BOY.

AS I TIPPY-TIPPY TOE THROUGH THE TREE TOPS,
I TAPPY-TAPPY…

> (Embarrassingly long silence as the battery on the iPhone player dies. The **CHORUS** exits. Bernie bangs at the iPhone player until he realizes the power cord is unplugged.

Hey! I hear the Major-General approaching the stage right now! Hide in this house and I'll appeal to his sense of decency.

SWEET CARNATION. Oh, great buckets of luck. And remember. Love is on our side!

> (**SWEET CARNATION** opens the door to the stage right house. **CHORUS BOY #1** runs out chased by **PATROLMAN #2** who thinks he's **JACKIE BALDO**. They exit downstage left **SWEET CARNATION** and the **NAUGHTY BOY** exchange a look. She exits into

the house. **JACKIE BALDO** *backs on from downstage right the* **NAUGHTY BOY** *sees him and runs off. Upstage left* **JACKIE BALDO** *sees the audience and runs off downstage right. From downstage left the* **MAJOR-GENERAL** *chases* **CHORUS GIRLS #1** *&* **#2.** *The* **GIRLS** *exit. The* **MAJOR-GENERAL** *calls after.)*

MAJOR-GENERAL Come back, maidens. Well. No matter. I'll catch you sooner or later. I always do.

MUSIC CUE #18: "IT'S ALL IN THE CHASE"

IT'S ALL IN THE CHASE
AND THE CHASE IS THE FUN.
IT'S NO FUN TO WALK
BUT IT'S SURE FUN TO RUN.
BUT ONCE THE RACE ENDS,
AND THE WOMAN IS YOURS.
IT ISN'T THE GIRL,
IT'S THE CHASE YOU ADORE.
I LOOK FOR A CHALLENGE,
AS MANY MEN DO.
AS YOU'LL SEE WHEN I SAY
WHAT I'M SAYING TO YOU.
I BATTLED BETTY'S BUTLER,
FOR A BIT OF BETTY'S BOTTOM.
BUT BETTY'S BITTER BUTLER,
BEAT ME BADLY WITH A PAIL.
SO BETTY MADE A BATTER OUT OF BUTTER,
BUT IT BURNED ME.
BUT THE BUTTER ON HER BOTTOM,
MADE A BETTER BIT OF TAIL.
MEETING MY MELBA IN MELBOURNE ON MONDAY,
I MET ME A MODEL – MISS MELANIE MOST.
MELANIE'S MELONS
MADE MELBA'S LOOK MANLY.
MOLESTING MY MODEL I MADE MELBA TOAST.
IT'S ALL IN THE CHASE
AND THE CHASE IS THE FUN.
IT'S NO FUN TO WALK

BUT IT'S SURE FUN TO RUN.
BUT ONCE THE RACE ENDS
AND THE WOMAN IS YOURS.
IT ISN'T THE GIRL,
IT'S THE CHASE YOU ADORE.

> (The **NAUGHTY BOY** *runs on, chased by* **JACKIE**
> **BALDO.** *The* **SERGEANT** *chases* **CHORUS BOY #2**
> *on from the other direction.* **JACKIE BALDO** *flees,*
> *the* **PATROLMEN** *follow, leaving the* **NAUGHTY**
> **BOY** *behind onstage to join in the song.*)

MAJOR-GENERAL

I LOOK FOR A CHALLENGE,
AS MANY MEN DO.
AS YOU'LL SEE WHEN I SAY
WHAT I'M SAYING TO YOU.

NAUGHTY BOY.

HOT-HEADED HEDDA HAD HEADY HOT HOOTERS.
I HADN'T HAD HOOTERS AS HEADY AS THAT.
I HEADED TO HEDDA TO HANDLE HER HOOTERS.
HER HOOTERS WERE HEAVY
AND SMOTHERED MY CAT.

MAJOR-GENERAL.

I WANTED TO WANDER ROWANDA WITH WANDA,
BUT WANDA WOULD WANDER
WITH WENDALL AND JUAN.
SO WANDA AND WENDALL
WENT YONDER TO WANDER,
WHILE JUAN WENT AT ME
AND WE BOTH GOT IT ON.

MAJOR-GENERAL & THE NAUGHTY BOY.

IT'S ALL IN THE CHASE
AND THE CHASE IS THE FUN.
IT'S NO FUN TO WALK
BUT IT'S SURE FUN TO RUN.
BUT ONCE THE RACE ENDS,
AND THE WOMAN IS YOURS
IT ISN'T THE GIRL.

IT'S THE CHASE YOU ADORE.

> (*The* **MAYOR** *enters, running from* **JACKIE BALDO***,*
> *the* **PATROLMEN** *come from the other side, chase*
> *him off and the* **MAYOR** *joins in, as well.*)

I LOOK FOR A CHALLENGE, AS MANY MEN DO.
AS YOU'LL SEE WHEN I SAY
WHAT I'M SAYING TO YOU.

MAYOR.

CHUCK CHASED A CHARMER,
WITH CHOCOLATE AND CHEESECAKE,
AND CHUTNEY AND CHOWDER,
AND CHUNKS OF CHOPPED CHEESE.
SHE CHEWED AS SHE CHOMPED,
AND HER CHUB CHANGED TO CHUNKS,
THEN HER CHEEKS CHOKED MY CHICKEN,
AND CHAPPED BOTH MY KNEES.

MAJOR-GENERAL.

PENELOPE PORTER HAS PURPOSELY PASSED ME.
PERTURBED AT MY PISTOL AND PENCHANT FOR PUNCH.

NAUGHTY BOY.

I PESTERED AND PLEADED
AND PRODDED WHEN NEEDED.

MAYOR.

HER PETTICOATS PARTED AND PILED IN A BUNCH.

ALL.

IT'S ALL IN THE CHASE
AND THE CHASE IS THE FUN.
IT'S NO FUN TO WALK
BUT IT'S SURE FUN TO RUN.
BUT ONCE THE RACE ENDS
AND THE WOMAN IS YOURS.
IT ISN'T THE GIRL,
IT'S THE CHASE YOU ADORE.

> (**THE FOOL** *enters chased by* **JACKIE BALDO***. The*
> **SERGEANT** *enters chasing after* **JACKIE BALDO***.*
> **THE FOOL** *stays behind and joins in the song.*)

I LOOK FOR A CHALLENGE,
AS MANY MEN DO.
AS YOU'LL SEE WHEN I SAY
WHAT I'M SAYING TO YOU.

THE FOOL.

I SLEEP WITH A SHEEP,
OUR CHEEKS ON CHEAP SHEETS.
IT'S SWEET IN THE SHEETS,
AS SHE KEEPS MY MEAT WARM.
SHE BLEATS, LEAPS AND WEEPS,
AND SHE SMELLS UP THE SHEETS.
I DON'T CARE WHAT YOU PREACH...
ANY PORT IN A STORM.

MAJOR-GENERAL.

PICKLED,
I PICKED PATTY PETERS FOR PETTING.

NAUGHTY BOY.

FOR PETTING,
I PICKED PATTY PETERS TO BOINK.

MAYOR.

THE PROBLEM WITH PICKING
PAT PETERS FOR PETTING,
WAS PATTY'S PET PENCHANT
TO PIDDLE AND OINK.

ALL.

IT'S ALL IN THE CHASE
AND THE CHASE IS THE FUN.
IT'S NO FUN TO WALK
BUT IT'S SURE FUN TO RUN.
BUT ONCE THE RACE ENDS
AND THE WOMAN IS YOURS.
IT ISN'T THE GIRL,
IT'S THE CHASE YOU ADORE.
I LOOK FOR A CHALLENGE, AS MANY MEN DO.
AS YOU'LL SEE WHEN I SAY
WHAT I'M SAYING TO YOU.
THE MEN TAKE A VERY BIG BREATH.
I BATTLED BETTY'S BUTLER,

FOR A BIT OF BETTY'S BOTTOM.
BUT BETTY'S BITTER BUTLER,
BEAT ME BADLY WITH A PAIL.
SO BETTY MADE A BATTER OUT OF BUTTER,
BUT IT BURNED ME.
BUT THE BUTTER ON HER BOTTOM,
MADE A BETTER BIT OF TAIL.
MEETING MY MELBA IN MELBOURNE ON MONDAY,
I MET ME A MODEL – MISS MELANIE MOST.
MELANIE'S MELONS
MADE MELBA'S LOOK MANLY.
MOLESTING MY MODEL I MADE MELBA TOAST.
HOT-HEADED HEDDA HAD HEADY HOT HOOTERS.
I HADN'T HAD HOOTERS AS HEADY AS THAT.
I HEADED TO HEDDA TO HANDLE HER HOOTERS.
HER HOOTERS WERE HEAVY
AND SMOTHERED MY CAT.
I WANTED TO WANDER ROWANDA WITH WANDA,
BUT WANDA WOULD WANDER
WITH WENDALL AND JUAN.
SO WANDA AND WENDALL
WENT YONDER TO WANDER,
WHILE JUAN WENT AT ME
AND WE BOTH GOT IT ON.
CHUCK CHASED A CHARMER,
WITH CHOCOLATE AND CHEESECAKE,
AND CHUTNEY AND CHOWDER,
AND CHUNKS OF CHOPPED CHEESE.
SHE CHEWED AS SHE CHOMPED,
AND HER CHUB CHANGED TO CHUNK,
THEN HER CHEEKS CHOKED MY CHICKEN,
AND CHAPPED BOTH MY KNEES.
PENELOPE PORTER HAS PURPOSELY PASSED ME.
PERTURBED AT MY PISTOL AND PENCHANT FOR PUNCH.
I PESTERED AND PLEADED
AND PRODDED WHEN NEEDED.
HER PETTICOATS PARTED AND PILED IN A BUNCH.
I SLEEP WITH A SHEEP,
OUR CHEEKS ON CHEAP SHEETS.
IT'S SWEET IN THE SHEETS,

AS SHE KEEPS MY MEAT WARM.
SHE BLEATS, LEAPS AND WEEPS,
AND SHE SMELLS UP THE SHEETS.
I DON'T CARE WHAT YOU PREACH...
ANY PORT IN A STORM.
PICKLED,
I PICKED PATTY PETERS FOR PETTING.
FOR PETTING,
I PICKED PATTY PETERS TO BOINK.
THE PROBLEM WITH PICKING
PAT PETERS FOR PETTING,
WAS PATTY'S PET PENCHANT
TO PIDDLE AND OINK.
WE LOOK FOR A CHALLENGE,
AS MANY MEN DO.
AS YOU SAW WHEN WE SAID,
WHEN WE SAID IT TO YOU.
WHEN WE SAID IT TO YO-OU!

> *(They take a bow [and a much needed breath].* **JACKIE BALDO** *chases* **CHORUS GIRLS** *and a terrified stage hand across the stage. Everyone panics and scatters.* **SWEET CARNATION'S NAN** *enters from her house stage right still in character.)*

SWEET CARNATION'S NAN. *(Crossing between the* **MAYOR** *and the* **MAJOR-GENERAL***)* Well, bless me big round butt cheeks... I...

> *(The* **SERGEANT** *runs on stage left to stage right banging into* **SWEET CARNATION'S NAN***, the* **NAUGHTY BOY** *and the* **MAJOR-GENERAL***. They all fall to the ground on top of each other. The* **SERGEANT** *chases* **JACKIE BALDO** *from upstage right to downstage left the* **MAJOR-GENERAL** *rises, helmet-less. The* **NAUGHTY BOY** *pulls the point of the* **MAJOR-GENERAL***'s helmet out of his butt. The* **SERGEANT** *chases* **JACKIE BALDO** *from upstage left to upstage right. The* **NAUGHTY BOY** *and the* **MAJOR-GENERAL** *see them coming and scramble*

offstage. **SWEET CARNATION'S NAN** *is laid out flat on her back, unable to get up.)*

A little 'elp. A little 'elp, please.

(A **PATROLMAN** *chases* **CHORUS BOYS** *downstage left to downstage right, stepping over* **SWEET CARNATION'S NAN** *'s stomach.)*

A little 'elp, please.

(A stage hand dressed in black comes out and drags her off. **THE FOOL** *runs on.)*

PETEY (THE FOOL). Hide me. Hide me. He's crazy. Is anyplace safe?

(He opens the door to the house stage left revealing **MICKEY** *(the* **NAUGHTY BOY***) and two half dressed* **CHORUS GIRLS** *groping each other.)*

MICKEY (NAUGHTY BOY). Shut the door.

*(***THE FOOL** *closes the door.* **PATROLMAN #2** *runs on after him.)*

PETEY (THE FOOL). Look. Please. I told you. I'm not Jackie Baldo. What are you chasing me for?

PATROLMAN #2. I can't help it. I like you.

(From the stage right house, **SWEET CARNATION** *clogs on again to do her line.)*

SWEET CARNATION. What ho... I...

*(***SWEET CARNATION'S NAN** *crosses by screaming, upstage left to upstage right, with a dog chewing at her sleeve.* **SWEET CARNATION** *backs up and re-enters.)*

What ho... I...

(In the audience, we hear:)

SERGEANT. I got him! I got him!

(The **SERGEANT** *beats the crap out of an unsuspecting audience member. the* **PATROLMEN** *pop their heads out from backstage to watch.)*

What? Oh. Sorry, sir. Enjoy the show.

> *(To actors)*

Sorry. Shit.

> *(He exits. The two* **PATROLMEN** *laugh at him and exit backstage.)*

SWEET CARNATION. What ho… I…

> *(Suddenly, from the stage left house – the* **NAUGHTY BOY** *and the two half dressed* **CHORUS GIRLS** *are chased out of the house by* **JACKIE BALDO***. They exit downstage right.)*

SWEET CARNATION. What hoes.

> *(***JACKIE BALDO** *hears her and stops his exit. He turns back to* **SWEET CARNATION***.)*

JACKIE BALDO. There you are.

> *(***JACKIE BALDO** *chases* **SWEET CARNATION** *into the stage right house just as the* **NAUGHTY BOY***, the* **MAYOR** *and the* **GIRLS** *run on from upstage right. The* **GIRLS** *keep running off downstage left the* **MAYOR** *and the* **NAUGHTY BOY** *stay behind.)*

COREY (SWEET CARNATION). Nyaah. Help me, somebody!

CHUCK (MAYOR)/MICKEY (NAUGHTY BOY). Police! Over here!

> *(From backstage, the* **PATROLMEN** *enter with donuts.)*

PATROLMAN #2. Yeah?

CHUCK (MAYOR)/MICKEY (NAUGHTY BOY). He's in there!/ In there!

> *(***JACKIE BALDO** *pops out from the balcony, with* **COREY** *held as a hostage, shooting at the* **PATROLMEN***. The* **PATROLMEN** *shoot at* **JACKIE BALDO***. He shoots back. The* **MAYOR** *and the* **NAUGHTY BOY** *dodge bullets running back and forth two or three times. From the orchestra pit we hear:)*

BERNIE LUDLOE. Stop ruining my play!

> (*Sound Effects: "Three Gun Blasts."*)

> (**JACKIE BALDO** *shoots* **BERNIE** *in the shoulder.*)

JACKIE BALDO. Out of bullets!

MICKEY (NAUGHTY BOY). He's out of bullets!

PATROLMAN #2. Well, he's not getting any of mine.

MICKEY (NAUGHTY BOY). Go after him!

PATROLMAN #2. Oh.

> (**JACKIE BALDO** *ducks back inside. The* **PATROLMEN** *charge the stage right house.*)

SERGEANT. Back, men. Damn, It's locked!

PATROLMAN #1. What should we do?

SERGEANT. Beats me.

> (*The* **PATROLMAN** *pistol whips him.*)

I said "beats me." Not "beat me."

PATROLMAN #1. Oh.

PATROLMAN #2. I saw a ladder back there.

SERGEANT. Get it!

> (*The* **SERGEANT** *and the* **PATROLMEN** *exit.*)

MICKEY (NAUGHTY BOY). Why don't you just go around the back of the house?

> (**MICKEY** *(the* **NAUGHTY BOY***) turns to realize he and* **CHUCK** *(the* **MAYOR***) are alone onstage. They both turn to see the audience, pause a beat and simultaneously do a time step to kill time. The* **PATROLMEN** *return with a ladder.* **CHUCK** *(the* **MAYOR***) and* **MICKEY** *(the* **NAUGHTY BOY***) duck under it. The* **PATROLMEN** *circle back just as* **CHUCK** *(the* **MAYOR***) rises again and gets clocked in the face. He flies backwards into the backdrop and collapses to the floor like a dead man.* **MICKEY** *(the* **NAUGHTY BOY***) rises, looking back at* **CHUCK** *(the* **MAYOR***) smugly, just in time to get hit in*

the face with the ladder as well. He flies into the proscenium arch and collapses.)

(As the **PATROLMEN** *climb the ladder,* **LORETTA** *(***SWEET CARNATION'S NAN***) rolls by at fast speed from stage right to stage left screaming – tangled in the legs of a rabid police dog.)*

(Sound Effects: "Snarling Dog.")

(The **PATROLMEN** *climb into the window through the balcony.* **CHUCK** *[the* **MAYOR***] rises, feeling his bloody nose from the ladder. The* **PATROLMEN** *return from the stage right house.)*

PATROLMAN #1. Lost him!

(They grab the ladder and exit upstage left cracking **CHUCK'***s nose a second time as they pass.)*

(Sound Effects: "Cracking Nose.")

(As **CHUCK** *[the* **MAYOR***] flies into the backdrop again and crumbles to the ground,* **CHORUS GIRL #2** *runs by chased by the* **MAJOR-GENERAL** *who is chased by* **THE FOOL.***)*

THE FOOL. What were you doing with that girl? Looking for Piccadilly Circus?

MAJOR-GENERAL. Showing her Big Ben.

(They run off. **JACKIE BALDO** *enters with* **COREY** *[***SWEET CARNATION***] over his shoulder and carrying a gun.)*

COREY (SWEET CARNATION). Put me down!

(The **SERGEANT** *enters the opposite side.)*

SERGEANT. Okay. Let's just take it easy.

(slowly lowering his gun to the floor)

Look, Jackie. I'm dropping my gun so we can speak.

(kicking his gun over to **JACKIE BALDO***)*

See? I have no gun.

JACKIE BALDO. Then you're an idiot.

> *(***JACKIE BALDO*** *picks up the* **SERGEANT** *'s gun.)*

Dance.

SERGEANT. Come on, now. This isn't some old movie where...

JACKIE BALDO. Dance.

> *(***JACKIE BALDO*** *shoots the gun at the* **SERGEANT** *'s feet. The* **SERGEANT** *does a time-step, dances the cabbage patch, and moonwalks backwards.)*

> *(to* **COREY/SWEET CARNATION***)* You're coming with me.

> *(***MICKEY** *[***NAUGHTY BOY***] crawls offstage left.)*

COREY (SWEET CARNATION). What are you going to do to me?

JACKIE BALDO. Everything.

COREY (SWEET CARNATION). Oh, God! No! Bernie, help me.

BERNIE. *(using an audience member as a human shield)* Stay in character.

MICKEY (NAUGHTY BOY). *(Offstage left)* I'll save you!

> *(The* **NAUGHTY BOY** *swings in on a rope from stage left in his pirate shirt & headband, just as the* **MAYOR** *wakes up and starts to cross downstage. Instead of landing on* **JACKIE BALDO***, the* **NAUGHTY BOY** *kicks the* **MAYOR** *in the face, sending him flying offstage.* **LORETTA** *[***SWEET CARNATION'S NAN***] enters stage left to see the* **NAUGHTY BOY** *flying back off right at her. She runs off stage left as his rope swings off stage left. We hear a crashing offstage.)*

> *(Sound Effects: "Offstage Crash/Sweet Carnation's Nan's Screams/Dog Yelping.")*

JACKIE BALDO. *(to* **COREY***)* You're mine now.

COREY (SWEET CARNATION). Somebody do something!

> *(***BERNIE** *fires a pistol.)*

(Sound Effects: "Loud Shot.")

*(The shot gets **JACKIE BALDO** in the leg. He goes down on a knee, releasing **SWEET CARNATION**. The **PATROLMEN** seize him. Silence.)*

BERNIE. Now finish my play!

SERGEANT. Okay, okay, Bernie! Take it easy. You have no idea how dangerous this man is.

COREY (SWEET CARNATION). What exactly did he do, Sergeant?

SERGEANT. Murder. Horrible cold-blooded murder. Off the coast of Asbury Park about twenty years ago, Jackie Baldo threw two innocent people off the side of a little dingy boat and kidnapped their newborn baby.

MICKEY (NAUGHTY BOY). Boy this story sounds familiar.

SERGEANT. The little baby was never found. Eyewitnesses claim he had an accomplice on the dock.

PETEY (THE FOOL). The little baby had an accomplice on the dock?

SERGEANT. Jackie Baldo had the accomplice on the dock. The baby worked alone.

PETEY (THE FOOL). Oh.

SERGEANT. But we could never make an I.D. And he's too crazy to talk.

COREY (SWEET CARNATION). Who was it, Johnny? Who made you do these terrible things?

*(**LORETTA** Peaman staggers on.)*

JACKIE BALDO. *(pointing to **SWEET CARNATION'S NAN**)* Her!

MICKEY (NAUGHTY BOY). Sweet Carnation's Nan?

CHUCK (MAYOR). Of course! Who else could it be?

SWEET CARNATION'S NAN. What?

CHUCK (MAYOR). It's so obvious. It has to be her. That would explain why she took Carnation in as her own. After the scabies-covered old crow helped murder Sweet Carnation's parents, the guilt was so overwhelming she raised the couple's only child.

LORETTA. Chuck, what are you talking about?

MICKEY (NAUGHTY BOY). That's right. And she admitted she was on the dock when she saw Carnation's parents bobbing in the briny!

SERGEANT. Is this true?

LORETTA. Well, yes. But…

BROCK (MAJOR-GENERAL). And I was onstage when she admitted she found a baby in the water hanging off her fishy smelling hook!

LORETTA. I had to admit that. It was in the script.

SERGEANT. You sick freak! You make me want to puke!

LORETTA. What's the matter with you? He's talking about fictional characters! How could I have killed fictional characters?

SERGEANT. You tell us! Let's go!

(The **SERGEANT** *starts to drag* **LORETTA** *away.)*

LORETTA. What are you talking about –

CHUCK (MAYOR). I'm so disappointed in you, Loretta.

(The **PATROLMEN** *handcuff her.)*

MICKEY (NAUGHTY BOY). How did you ever track them down to this theater, Sergeant?

(spotlight on the **SERGEANT** *)*

(as we hear:)

MUSIC CUE #19: "ON THE RUN OR ON THE LAM"

(A vamp begins. The **SERGEANT** *is confused.* **BERNIE** *cues him. He hesitates, then dives in with song.)*

SERGEANT.
ON THE RUN OR ON THE LAM…
IF YOU'VE A KILO OR A GRAM…
I'LL FIND YOUR BUTT.
OOPS. SORRY, MA'AM.

I ALWAYS, ALWAYS GET MY MAN...

PATROLMEN. *(Popping into spotlight)*

HE ALWAYS, ALWAYS GETS HIS MAN.

SERGEANT.

MY EYE IS KEEN AND SO'S MY NOSE...
TO HELP ME CATCH THE SO & SO'S...
AND IF YOU DON'T RESPECT THE CLOTHES...
I'LL BEAT YOU WITH MY RUBBER HOSE...

PATROLMEN.

HE'LL BEAT YOU WITH A RUBBER HOSE.

> *(Stage lights back up. The cast joins in the production number, marching, tapping and kicking.)*

ALL.

OH TO PRAISE THE MEN IN BLUE...
THEY KEEP THE STREETS SAFE JUST FOR YOU...
WHAT'S A HASSLE AND CURFEW?
IT'S BETTER HERE THAN KATMANDU...
ON THE RUN OR ON THE LAM...
WE SING THESE WORDS AD NAUSEAM...
FROM LIVERPOOL TO ROTTERDAM...
HE ALWAYS, ALWAYS GETS HIS MAN...

SERGEANT.

THAT'S WHAT I SA-ID

ALL. *(Except* **SERGEANT***)*

HE ALWAYS, ALWAYS GETS HIS MAN...

SERGEANT.

THAT'S WHAT I ME-AN.

ALL. *(Except* **SERGEANT***)*

HE ALWAYS, ALWAYS GETS HIS MAN...

SERGEANT.

OH ARE YOU LIST-NIN'?

ALL. *(Except* **SERGEANT***)*

OH, YES, WE AM... OH, YES, WE AM...

ALL.

HE (I). ALWAYS. GET(S). HIS (MY). MAN!

(Everyone bows and curtsies. The **SERGEANT**, *however, decides he'll do an unasked for encore.)*

SERGEANT.

IF IN THE CELL YOUR LIFE SHOULD END...
THAT SHOULD MAKE YOU COMPREHEND...
THERE'S NO ONE I CAN'T APPREHEND...
POLICEMEN ARE A MAN'S BEST FRIEND.

PATROLMEN.

THAT'S WHAT HE SA-ID.

ALL. *(Except* **PATROLMEN***)*

POLICEMEN ARE A MAN'S BEST FRIEND.

PATROLMEN.

THAT'S WHAT HE ME-ANS.

ALL. *(Except* **PATROLMEN***)*

POLICEMEN ARE A MAN'S BEST FRIEND.

PATROLMEN.

OH, ARE WE LISTNIN'?

SERGEANT.

POLICEMEN ARE... POLICEMEN ARE...

ALL.

POLICEMEN ARE, POLICEMEN ARE,
POLICEMEN ARE, POLICEMEN ARE,
A COP'S A MAN'S BEST FRIEND...
AND IF A STRANGER GOES NUTS,
JUST LOOK FOR DUNKIN' DONUTS.
A MAN'S BEST FRI—END...!

(Everyone bows.)

SERGEANT. Let's go, you psychopath!

(The cops drag **LORETTA** *and Johnny down the center aisle of the theater.)*

LORETTA. *(almost out the back door)* Chuck! Chuck! Do something!

CHUCK. I have to finish the show, Loretta. I'll see you...in twenty-five to life!

(In character as the **MAYOR***)*

Maybe fifteen for good behavior! Anyway...

MUSIC CUE #20: "ON THE RUN PLAYOFF MUSIC"

(The PATROLMEN, LORETTA, *and* JACKIE BALDO *exit. The actors wave goodbye. A beat, then the* MAYOR *starts the show again.)*

MAYOR. Anyway...where were we? Ah, who cares? Let's just cut to the chase, shall we? Back in my hamlet, will the Major-General let Sweet Carnation marry the Naughty Boy? Let us go see.

MAJOR-GENERAL. Sweet Carnation. You may marry the Naughty Boy, after all. There shall be no wedding between us this day.

SWEET CARNATION. Oh, Major-General. Do you mean to say that even a great warrior like you can never win in a battle against true love?

BROCK (MAJOR-GENERAL). No. That's not what I'm talkin' about at all.

COREY (SWEET CARNATION). What?

BROCK (MAJOR-GENERAL). Coming this close to death tonight, I realized...my life has been a farce. It's time to tell the world the truth. I'm going to come out and say it.

COREY (SWEET CARNATION). Huh? Say what?!

BROCK (MAJOR GENERAL). I just said it. I'm out. And in love!

COREY (SWEET CARNATION). With who?!

(The MAJOR-GENERAL *looks to* CHUCK *for support.)*

CHUCK (MAYOR). Don't look at me.

MICKEY (NAUGHTY BOY). Don't look at me.

PETEY (THE FOOL). Look at me. Please, God. Look at me.

BROCK (MAJOR-GENERAL). I love...the Fool.

BERNIE. *(Back at his conductor stand, script in hand)* No, you don't!

BROCK (MAJOR-GENERAL). Yes, I... I think I do.

PETEY (THE FOOL). Brock...?

BROCK (MAJOR-GENERAL). Petey...?

MICKEY (NAUGHTY BOY). Wait a second. When we rehearsed this thing, I married Sweet Carnation, you married Chorus Girl #1, and the Mayor married Sweet Carnation's Nan.

BROCK (MAJOR-GENERAL). Well, life is just full of little surprises, isn't it, Naughty Boy?

COREY (SWEET CARNATION). But, Fool.

THE FOOL. I'm not the Fool. I'm...

(Dramatic and proud)

I'm "Mrs. Major-General."

SWEET CARNATION. Then they can be married as well!

(Everyone cheers.)

NAUGHTY BOY. And so shall we!

(Everyone cheers.)

MAJOR-GENERAL. What about you, Mayor? Aren't you going to get married, too?

MAYOR. To who, stupid? My wife just got taken away to ja – ...

(Sees pretty CHORUS GIRLS)

Ya. Ya. I'll marry all you girls. If you'll have me. I'm a Mormon now.

(The CHORUS GIRLS and CHORUS BOY #2 cheer.)

Ya ya. And once again, everyone is happy in the Happy Hamlet of Himm.

(All cheer.)

SWEET CARNATION. O Joyous day of celebration! There's going to be three weddings.

MUSIC CUE #21: "FINALE (MEDLEY)"

ALL.
> THERE'S GOING TO BE THREE WEDDINGS,
> THREE WEDDINGS, THREE WEDDINGS,
> THERE'S GOING TO BE THREE WEDDINGS,
> AND TODAY'S THE DAY.

IN CASE YOU WERE FORGETTING,
FORGETTING, THE WEDDINGS,
THERE'S GOING TO BE THREE WEDDINGS,

MAYOR.

TWO ARE STRAIGHT. ONE'S GAY!

ALL.

THERE'S GOING TO BE THREE WEDDINGS,
AND THAT ENDS THE PLAY!

SWEET CARNATION.

ONCE UPON A TIME,
AND VERY LONG AGO,

MAJOR-GENERAL.

SOMEWHERE IN A DREAM,
WE'VE LOVED BEFORE, I KNOW,

CHORUS GIRLS.

IN A HEAVENLY GARDEN,
BEYOND THE MISTS OF TIME,
YOU HELD ME IN YOUR ARMS,
AND TOLD ME YOU WERE MINE.

**SWEET CARNATION/NAUGHTY BOY/MAJOR-GENERAL/
THE FOOL.**

YES, ONCE UPON A TIME,
ONE STARRY NIGHT OF BLUE,
WE DREAMED A DREAM OF LOVE,
AND NOW THAT DREAM COMES TRUE!

MAYOR.

ALWAYS SEE IT THROUGH UNTIL THE END.
AND IF YOUR WIFE'S FACE REALLY DOES OFFEND,
JUST BE CLEVER.
A LIFE IN JAIL SHE'LL SPEND.
AND ALWAYS SEE IT THROUGH TILL THE END.

MAJOR-GENERAL.

I DON'T CARE WHO KNOWS WHICH WAY I BEND.

(Spoken)

QUICHE AND SHOW TUNES!
ARE WHAT I INTEND!

THE FOOL.

NOW AND FOREVER,

YOU'LL BE MY SPECIAL FRIEND.

BOTH.

AND WE'LL ALWAYS SEE IT THROUGH

TILL THE END.

SWEET CARNATION.

SEXY ROLES CAN BRING YOU PSYCHO FANS..

OH, THE PRICE OF STARDOM.

NAUGHTY BOY. *(tossing hotel key to* **CHORUS GIRL #4***)*

NOT FOR ME. I'VE HAD ALL FOUR OF THEM.

CHORUS BOYS.

ROTTEN BASTARD SCHMUCK.

(Two lines of the song play. No one sings. Then:)

MAYOR.

LORETTA SANG THAT PART.

BUT NOW SHE'S IN THE PEN!

ALL.

MAKING LICENSE PLATES,

WITH LESBIANS.

ALWAYS SEE IT THROUGH UNTIL THE END

WHEN YOU DON'T KNOW HOW

THEN JUST PRETEND.

THERE'S NO GREATER MESSAGE

THAT WE CAN SEND,

THEN JUST TO SEE IT THROUGH

TILL THE END.

TEY TA RA BOOM. LA DEE DA DEE DEND.

TEY TA RA BOOM. LA DEE DA DE DEND.

ONE MORE TIME.

LET'S SING IT ONCE AGAIN.

AND ALWAYS SEE IT THROUGH TILL THE END.

TEY TA RA BOOM. LA DEE DA DEE DEND.

TEY TA RA BOOM. LA DEE DA DEE DEND.

ONE MORE TIME. MUCH LOUDER IF YOU CAN.

AND ALWAYS SEE IT THROUGH TILL THE END.

TEY TA RA BOOM. LA DEE DA DE DEND.

TEY TA RA BOOM. LA DEE DA DEE DEND.
ONE MORE TIME. JUST LIKE JERRY HER-MAN.
AND ALWAYS SEE IT THROUGH TILL THE END.
TEY TA RA BOOM. LA DEE DA DEE DEND.
TEY TA RA BOOM. LA DEE DA DEE DEND.
ONE LAST TIME.
WE WON'T SING THIS AGAIN.

> *(In the aisles, ushers wave* Lion King *birds-on-a-stick over the audience's heads.)*

AND ALWAYS SEE IT THROUGH.
ALWAYS SEE IT THROUGH.

> *(A cheesy version of* Phantom*'s chandelier swings down over the audience.)*

ALWAYS SEE IT THROUGH TILL THE END...

> *(A cheesy version of* Miss Saigon*'s helicopter descends over the stage right house.)*

ALWAYS SEE IT THROUGH TILL THE END...

> *(The american flag, balloons and santa claus join for the last lines.)*

ALWAYS SEE IT THROUGH TILL THE END...
ALWAYS SEE IT THROUGH TILL THE END...

> *(curtain)*

End of show

(curtain call)

MUSIC CUE #22: "CURTAIN CALL MUSIC"

(The curtain call is performed in character. **BERNIE** *conducts like a lunatic throughout. The* **PATROLMEN** *bow with their dogs.* **JACKIE BALDO** *bows — held at gunpoint by the* **SERGEANT***. On the final note, after the final bow, the stage left house crashes down on the star's head, his/her body passing through the break-away window on the second story a La Buster Keaton.)*

PROPERTY LIST

"Be on the Lookout" Flyers

iPhone Player with Speakers

Musical Score

Baton

Hard Candy (pebble)

Beer Steins (9+)

Play Program

Carnation Bower Hearts

Sandwich

Sword

Sheath

Guns (5)

Maypole

Wedding Bouquet (2)

Clip-on Mustache

Toothbrush

Souffle

Police dogs (2)

Club

Fog Machine

Night Stick

Donuts

Tall Ladder

Handcuffs

Birds on Stick (2)

American Flag

Cluster of Helium Balloons

COSTUME PLOT

LORETTA PEAMAN (SWEET CARNATION'S NAN)

    High collared blouse
    Full long skirt
    Eyelet bib apron
    Lace cap
    Fat suit with high density padding in front
    Black tights
    Character shoes

CHUCK PEAMAN (THE MAYOR)

    Bavarian style suit with knickers
    Peasant shirt with jabot and lace cuffs
    Over the knee socks
    Slip on dress shoes
    Bavarian cap with bright ostrich feather

MICKEY (THE NAUGHTY BOY)

    Cotton peasant shirt
    Lederhosen with embroidered suspenders
    Knee socks
    Hiking style boots
    Bavarian cap with very exaggerated bright ostrich feather
    Blond page-boy wig
    Satin peasant shirt
    Tight black dance pants or jeans
    Headband

COREY (SWEET CARNATION)

    Floral print dirndl
    Low cut peasant blouse
    Ribbons and flowers for hair
    Hooded dress length cape

BROCK (MAJOR-GENERAL)

    Red military uniform with medals
    Riding boots
    Pickelhaube (helmet)

PETEY (THE FOOL)

    Polka dot peasant shirt
    Lederhosen
    Knee socks

Hiking boots

Women's dirndl and blouse to match Corey (rigged for quick change)

Black stockings

Character shoes

Women's wig with bow to match Corey

SERGEANT TAGGERT

Police uniform

Police cap

Gun belt

TWO POLICEMEN

Police uniform

Police cap

Gun belt

BERNIE LUDLOE (CONDUCTOR)

Black frock coat

Tuxedo pants

Evening vest

Tux shirt

Poet tie

JACK "JACKIE" BALDO

Strait jacket

Black pants

Satin peasant shirt to match Mickey

Lederhosen, shirt, socks, boots, cap to match Mickey

CHORUS GIRLS

Full calico skirts with can-can ruffles underneath

Low cut peasant blouses

Black waist cincher

Black stockings

Character shoes

Flowers for hair

1 girl has black satin corselet, black briefs, rip-off version of skirt and blouse

CHORUS BOYS

Lederhosen with embroidered suspenders

Peasant shirt

White knee socks

Hiking boots

Bavarian cap with long feather

Also by
Billy Van Zandt, Jane Milmore, & Ed Alton

A Night At The Nutcracker (Musical)

Also by
Billy Van Zandt & Jane Milmore

Bathroom Humor

Confessions Of A Dirty Blonde

Do Not Disturb

Drop Dead!

Having A Wonderful Time, Wish You Were Her!

High School Reunion: The Musical

Infidelities!

Lie, Cheat, And Genuflect

A Little Quickie

Love, Sex, And The I.R.S.

Merrily We Dance And Sing (Musical)

The Pennies (Musical)

Playing Doctor

The Senator Wore Pantyhose

Silent Laughter

Suitehearts

Till Death Do Us Part

What The Bellhop Saw

What The Rabbi Saw

Wrong Window!

You've Got Hate Mail

Also by
Billy Van Zandt

The Property Known As Garland

VanZandtMilmore.com
SamuelFrench.com | SamuelFrench-London.co.uk